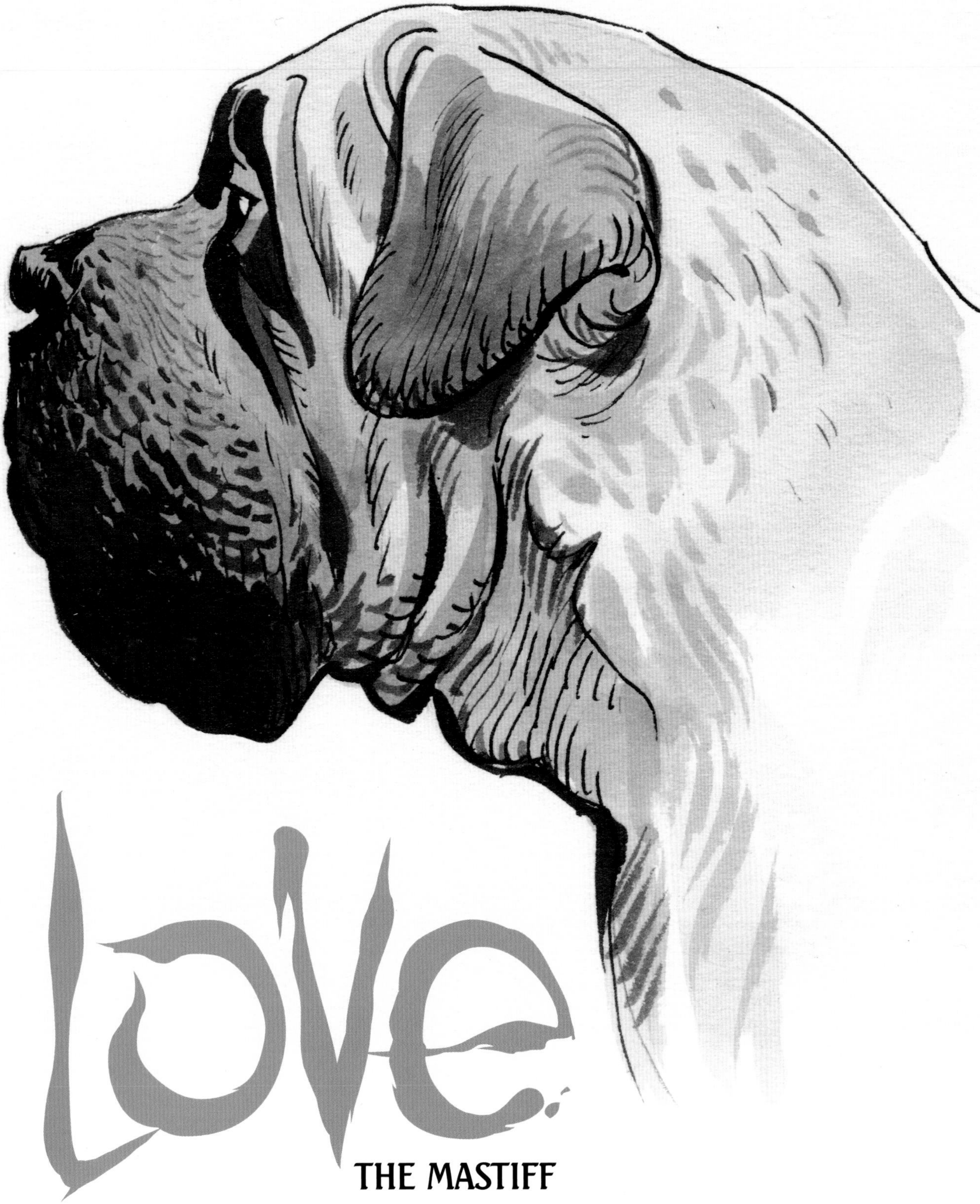

LOVE
THE MASTIFF

Frédéric Brrémaud Federico Bertolucci

MAGNETIC PRESS
www.MAGNETIC-PRESS.com

Written by **Frédéric Brrémaud**
Illustrated by **Federico Bertolucci**

Logo Design by Tony Derbomez

The LOVE series has been recognized for the following awards:

- LUCCA 2011 (Italy) - *Prix spécial du jury*
- ANGOULÊME 2012 (France) - *Sélection Prix BD des Collégiens*
- YALSA 2016 (USA) - *Selection Great Graphic Novels for Teens (The Tiger)*
- YALSA 2017 (USA) - *Selection Great Graphic Novels for Teens (The Fox)*
- YALSA 2018 (USA) - *Selection Great Graphic Novels for Teens (The Dinosaur)*
- INDEPENDENT PUBLISHERS AWARDS 2016 (USA) - *Gold Medal: Best Graphic Novel (The Fox)*
- EISNER AWARDS 2016 (USA) - *Federico Bertolucci: Best Painter/Multi-media artist (nominee)*
- EISNER AWARDS 2017 (USA) - *Best U.S. Edition of International Material (The Lion)*
- EISNER AWARDS 2017 (USA) - *Federico Bertolucci: Best Painter/Multi-media artist (nominee)*

Translation, Layout, and Editing by Mike Kennedy
Photos and clipart licensed from Envato

MAGNETIC™

ISBN: 978-1-951719-17-3

Library of Congress Control Number: 2021900809

Originally published as *Love: Le Molosse* © Editions Glénat 2021 by Brrémaud and Bertolucci. All rights reserved.

10 9 8 7 6 5 4 3 2 1

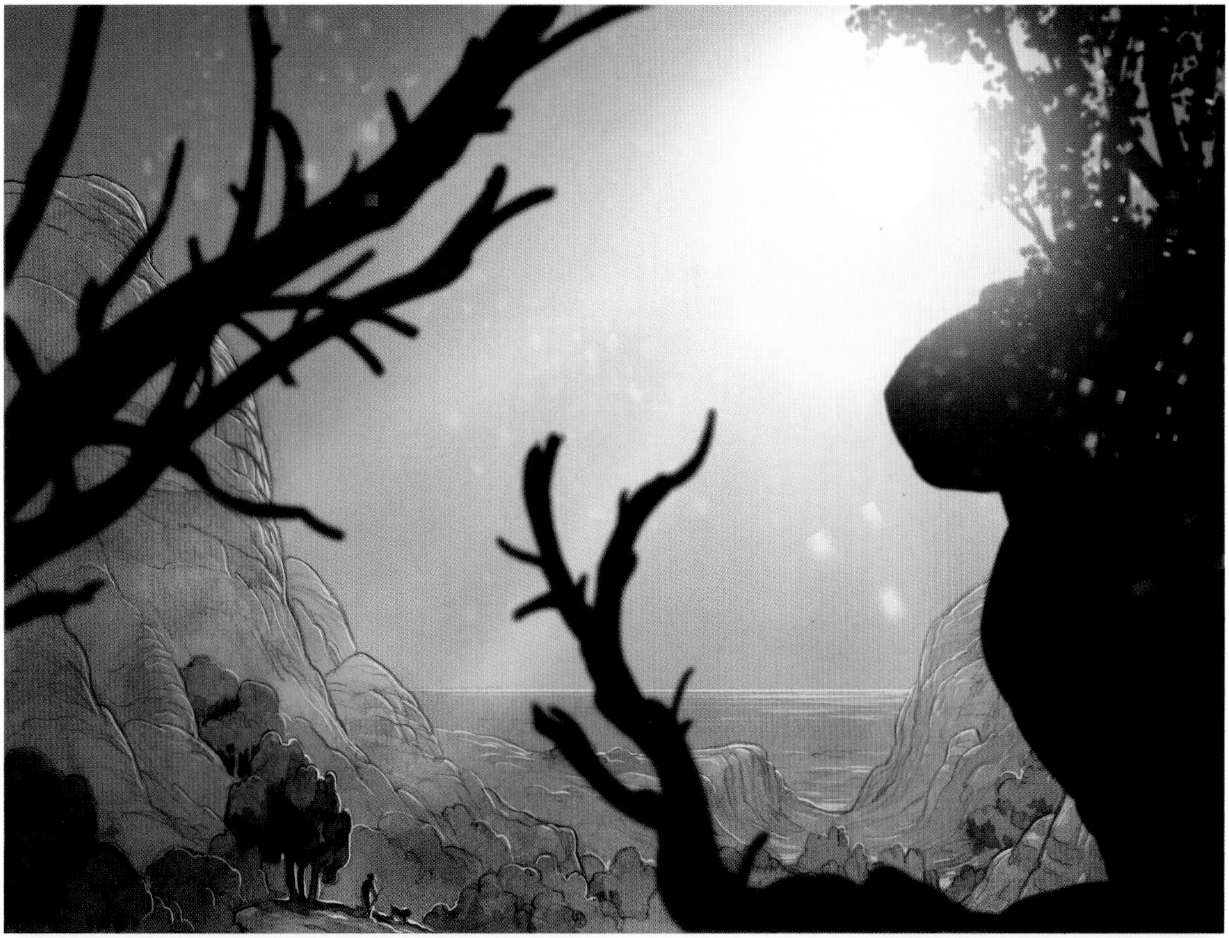
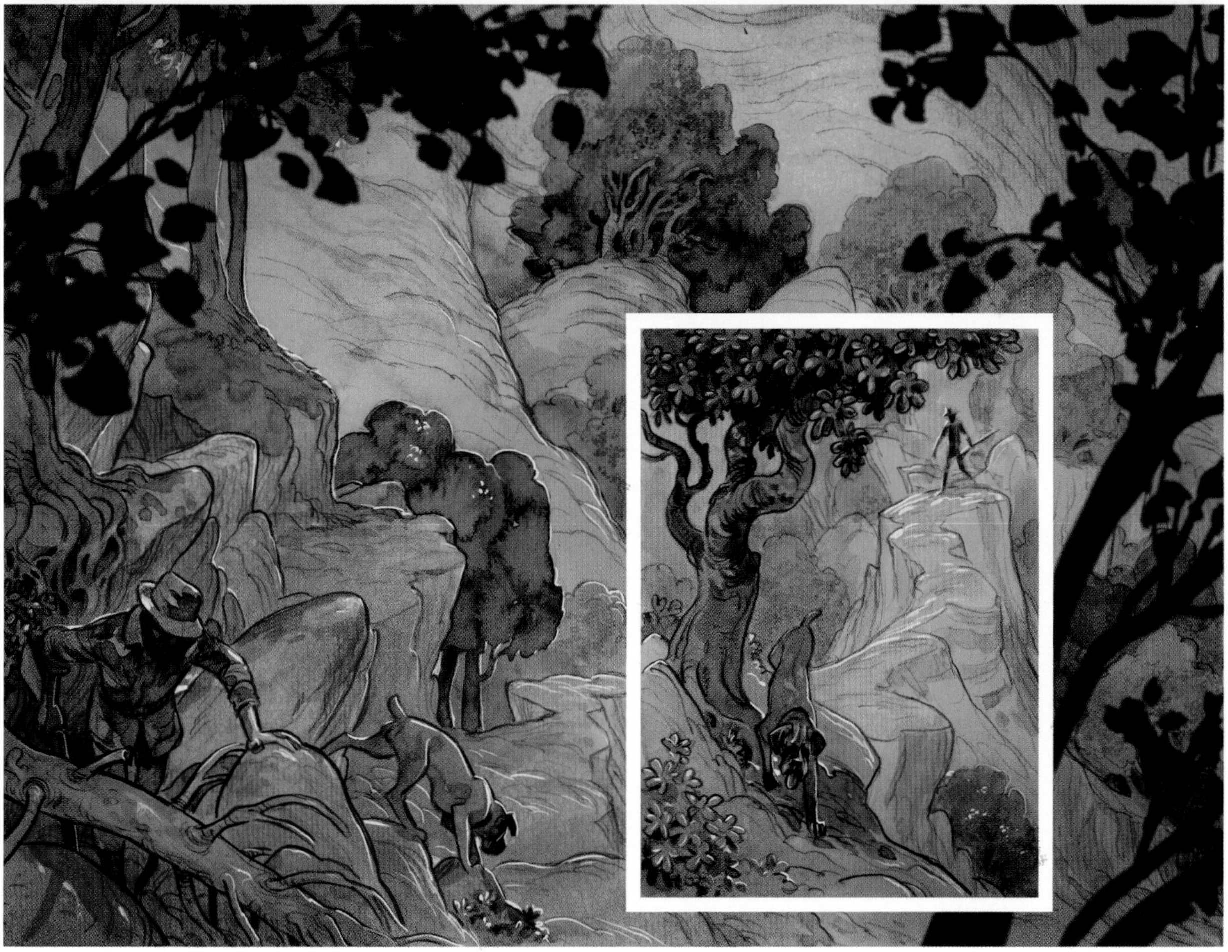

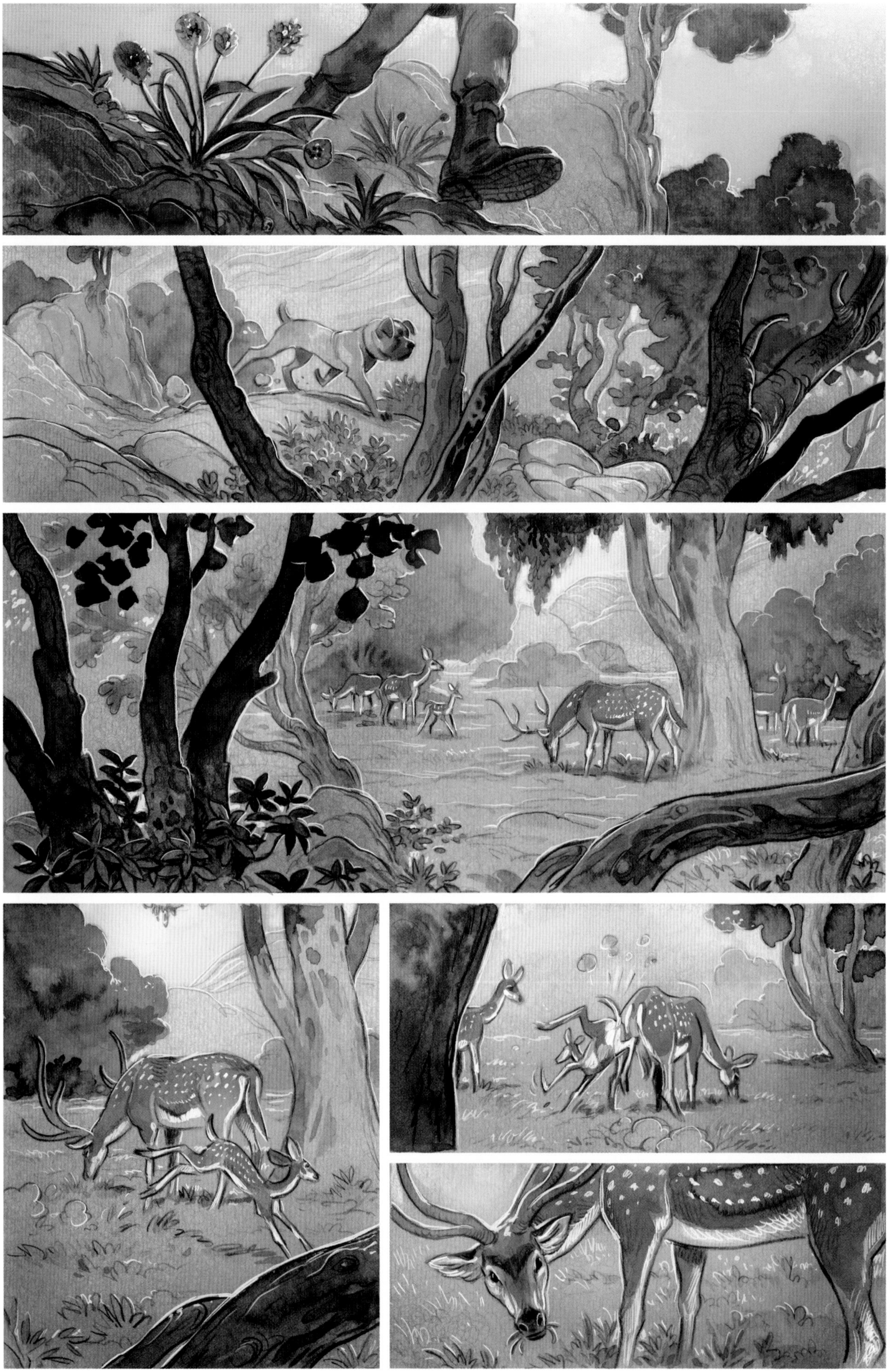

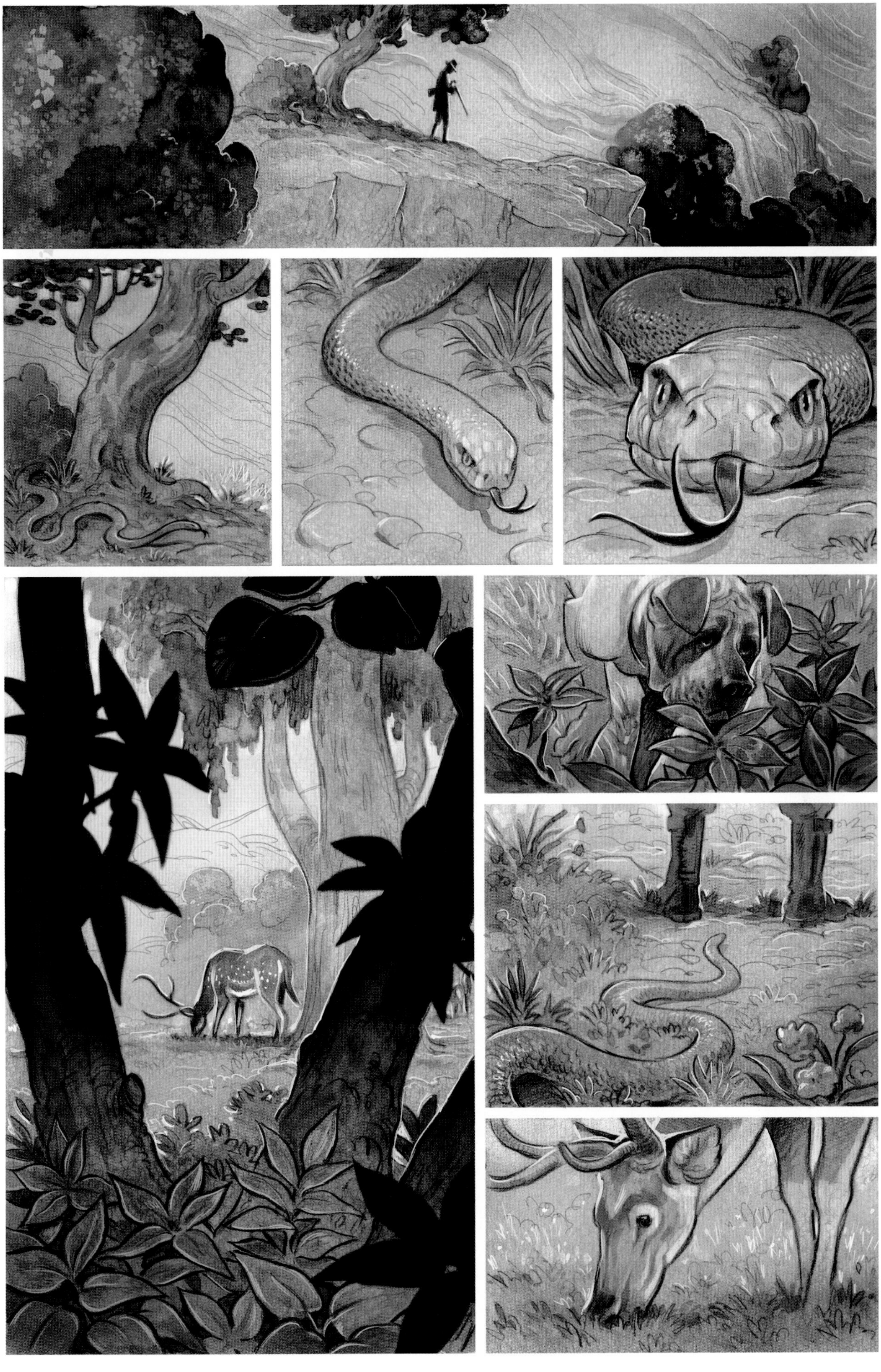

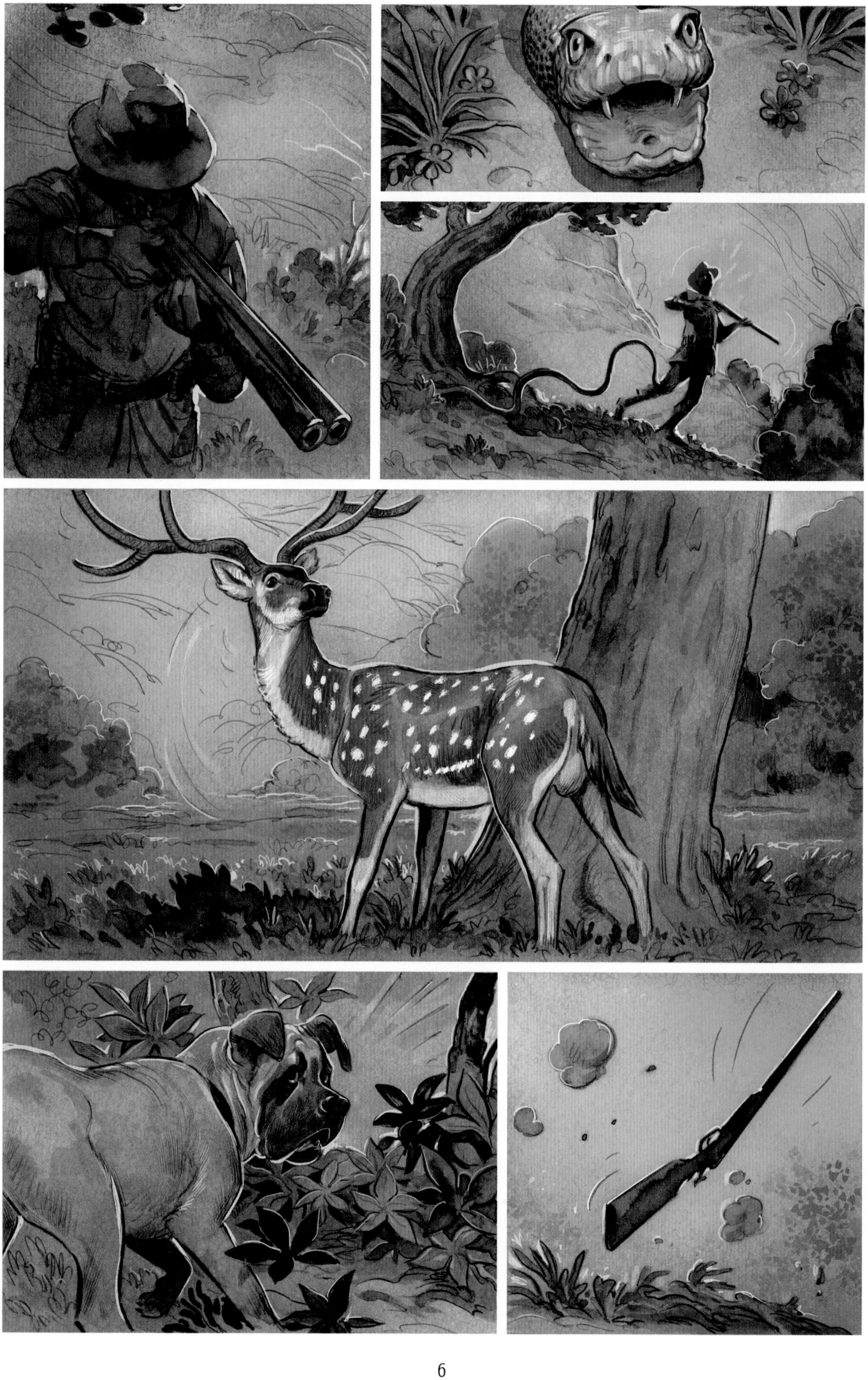

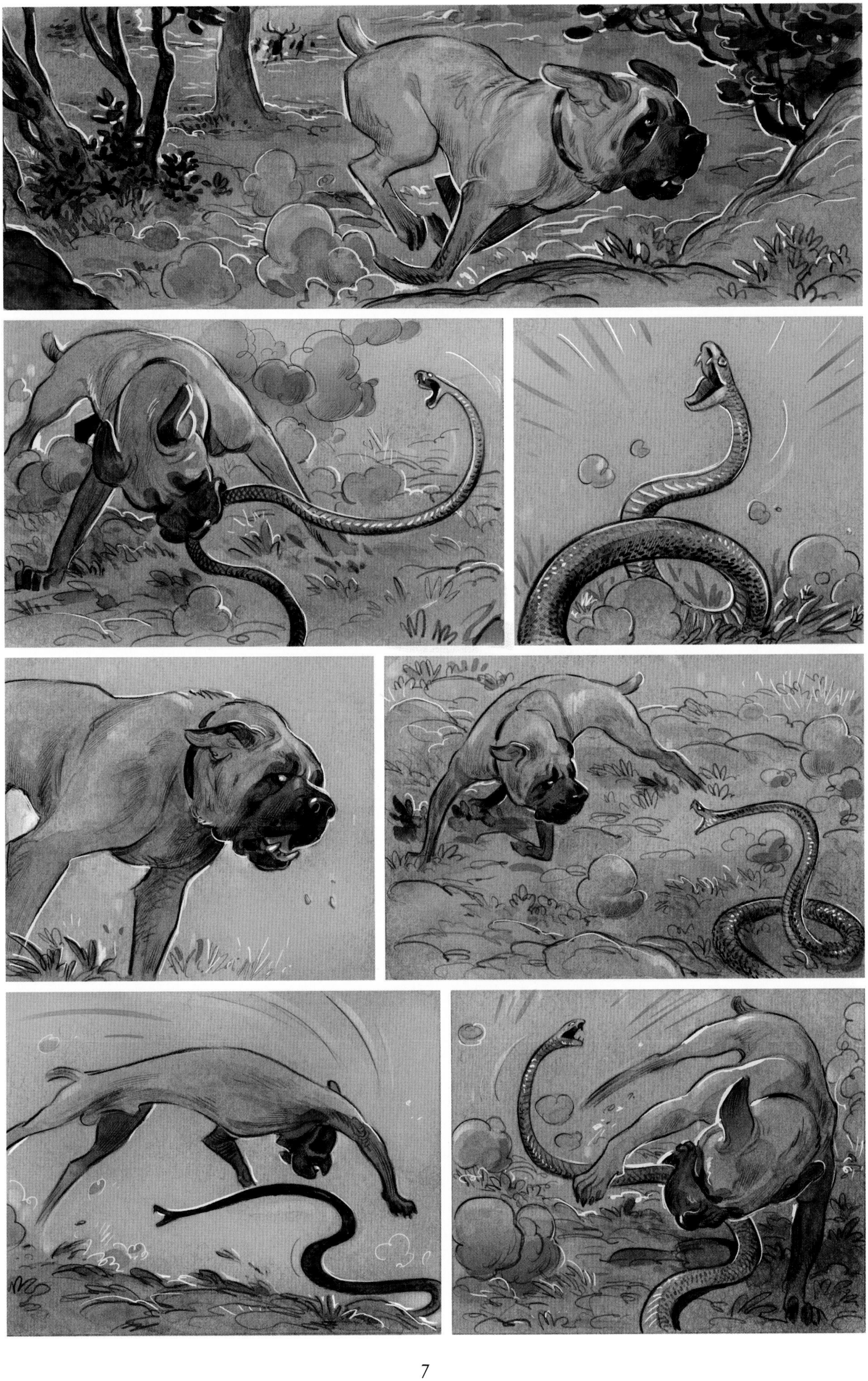

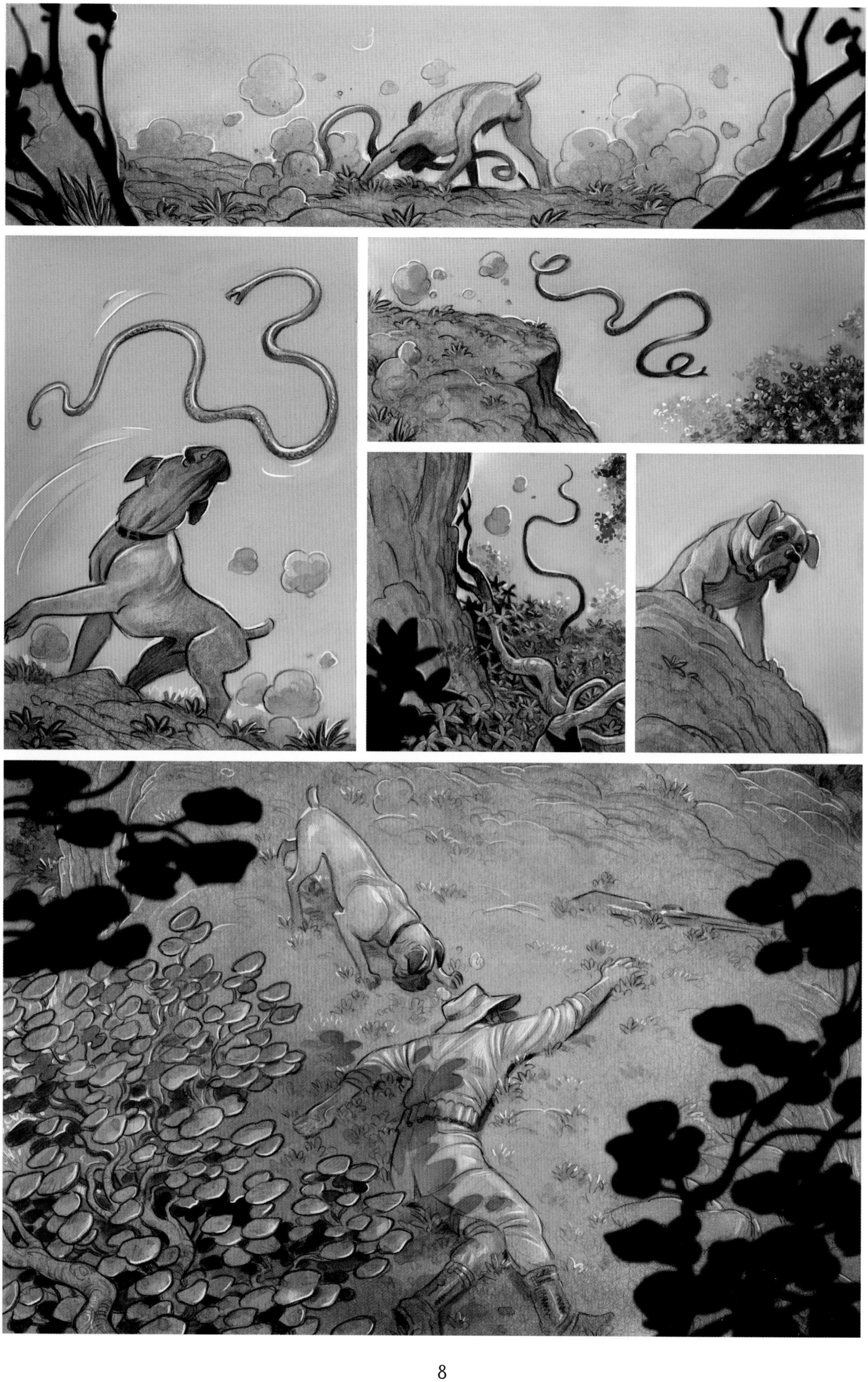

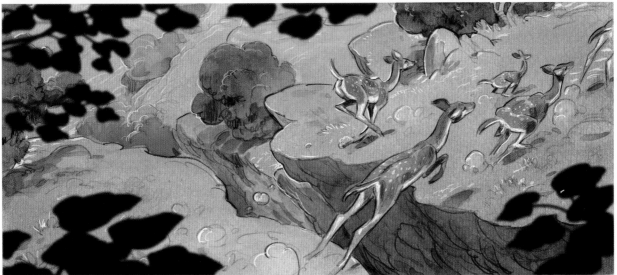

9

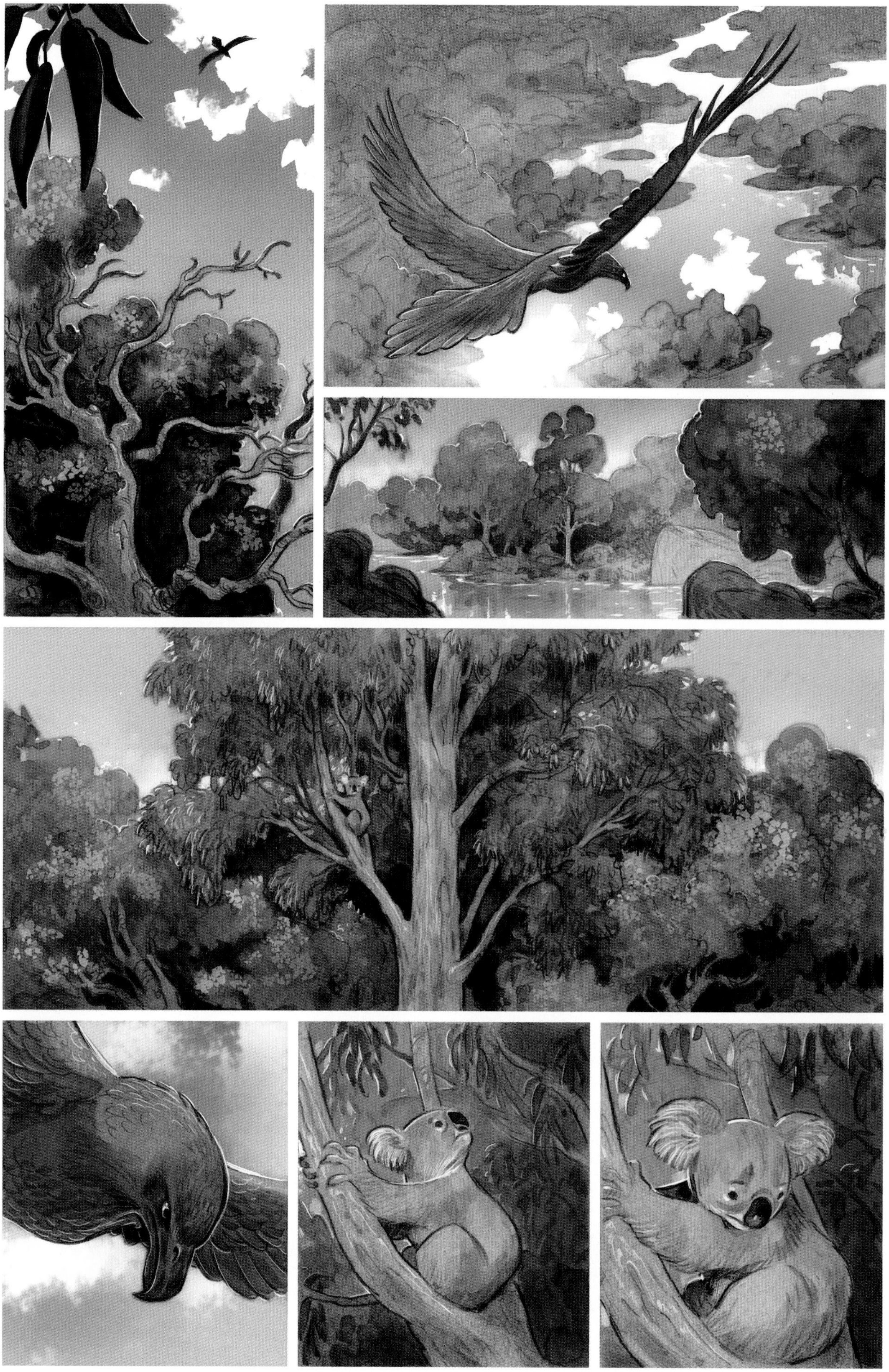

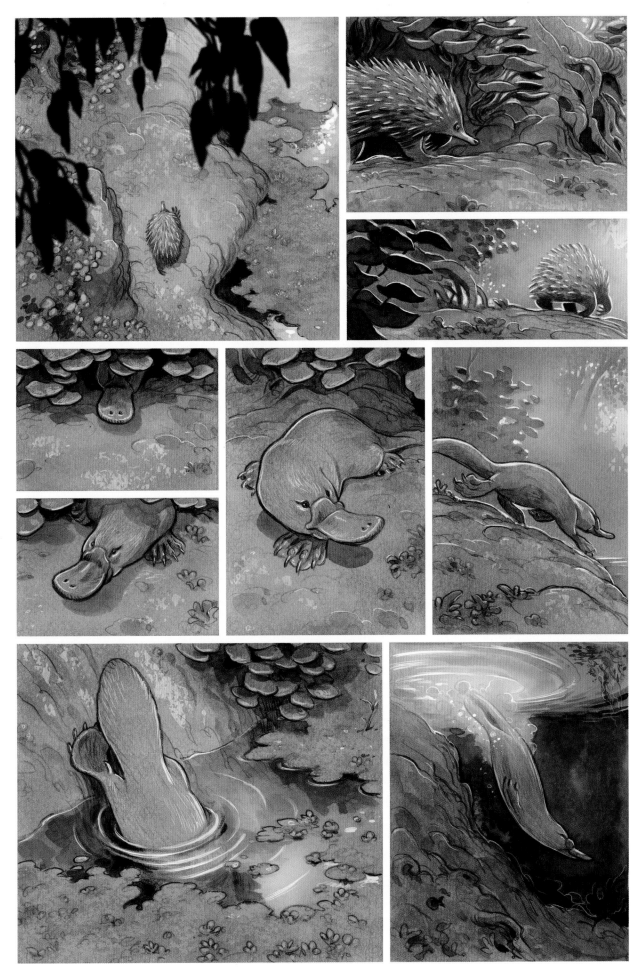

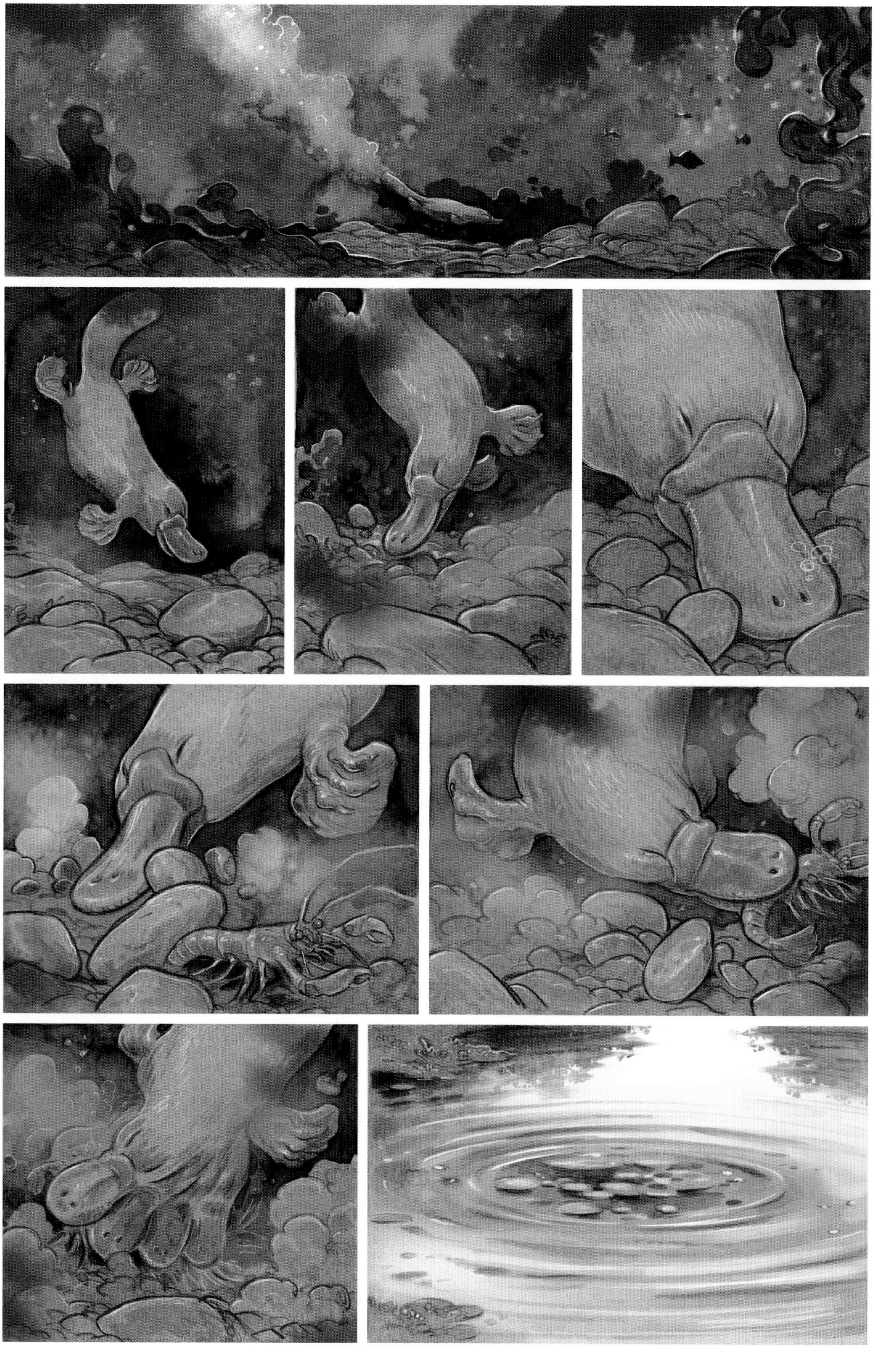

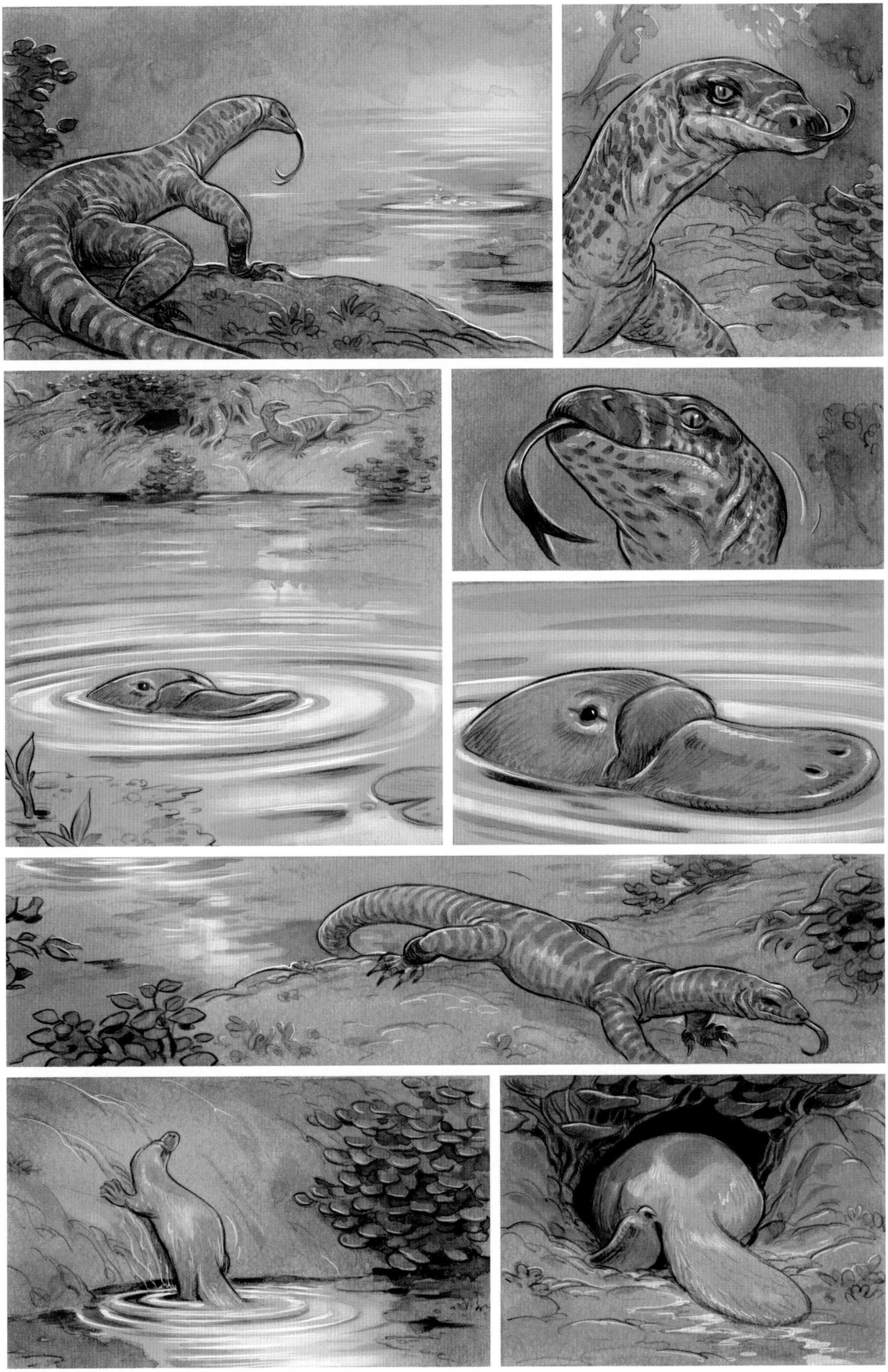

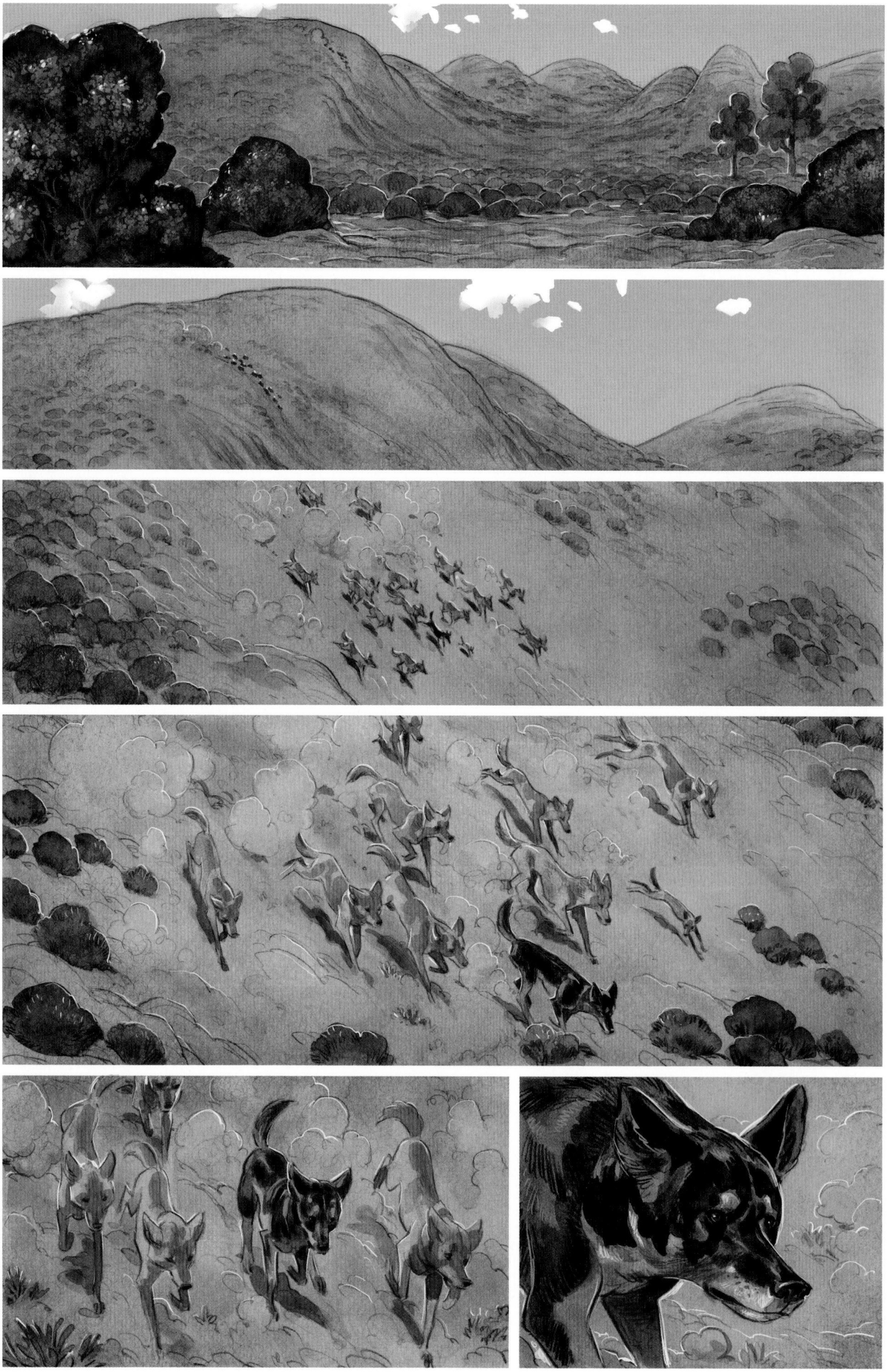

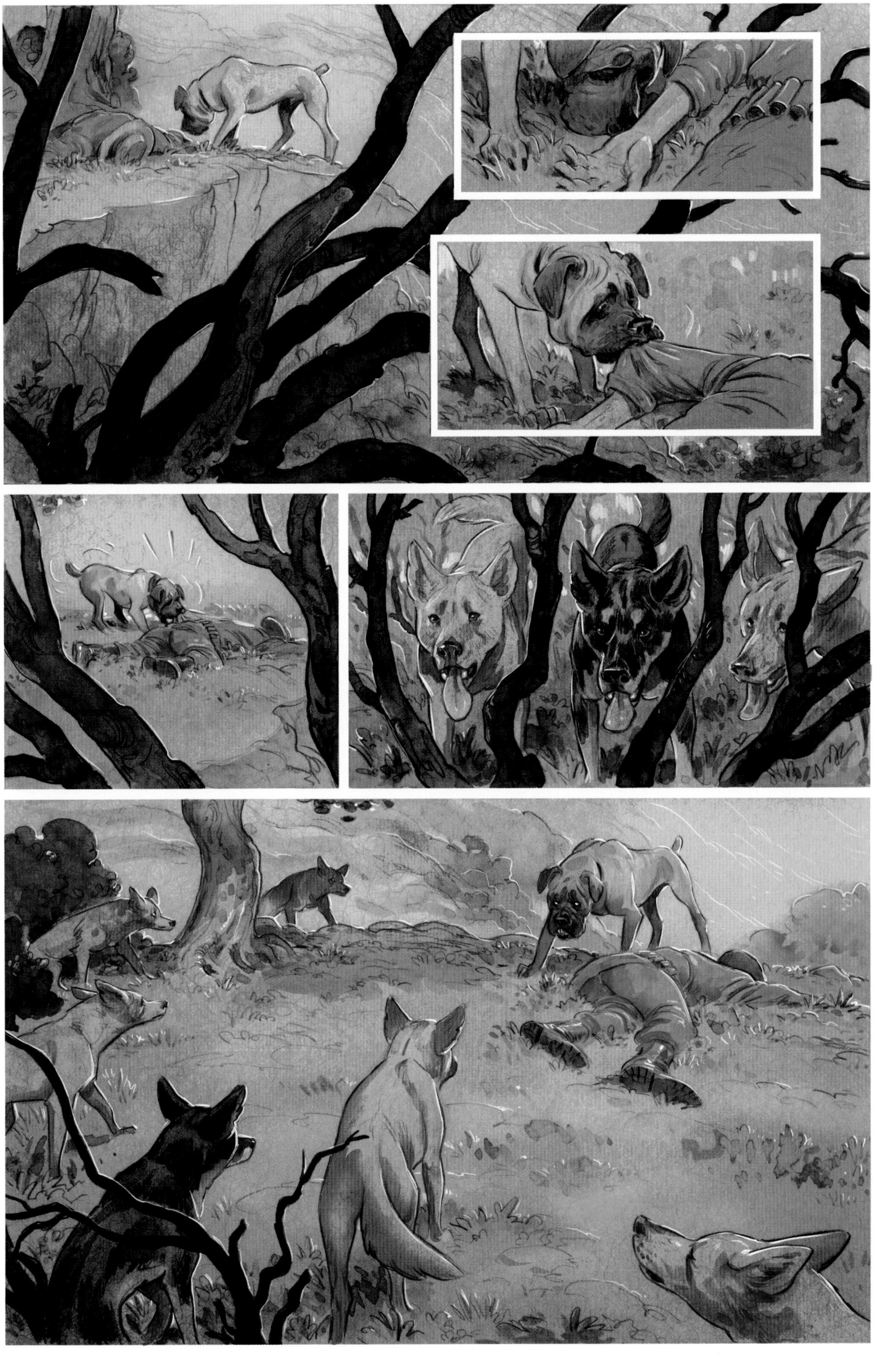

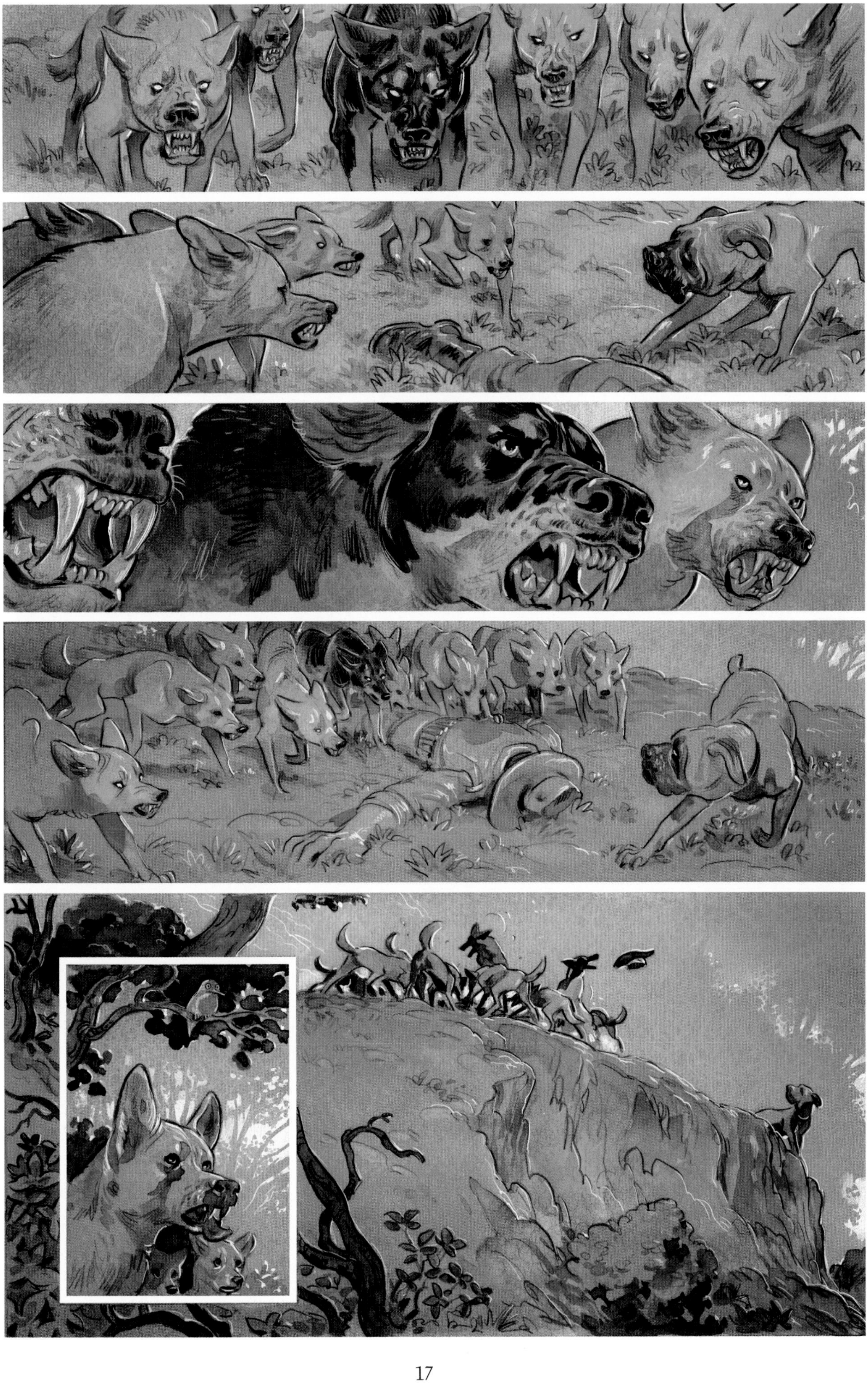

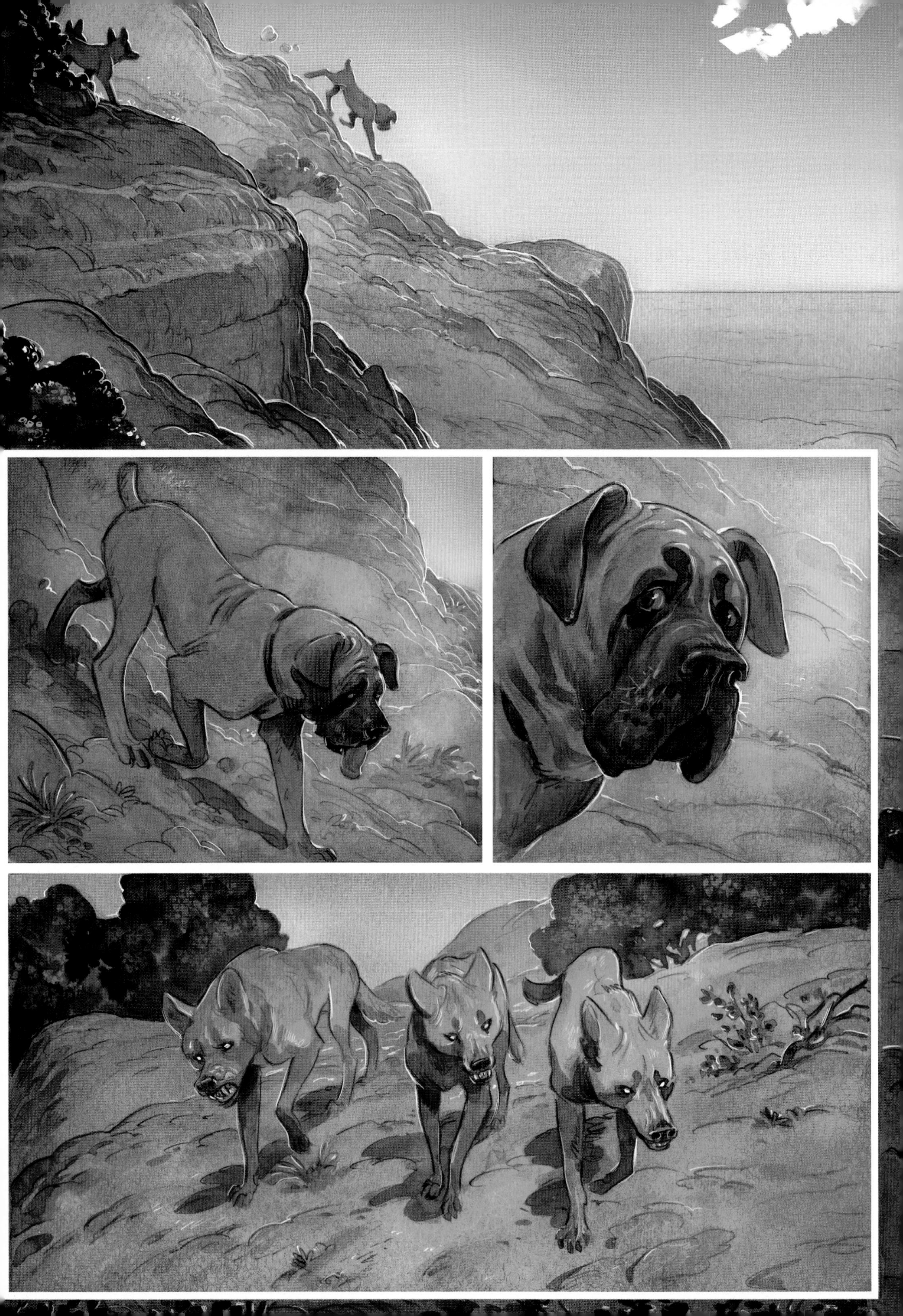

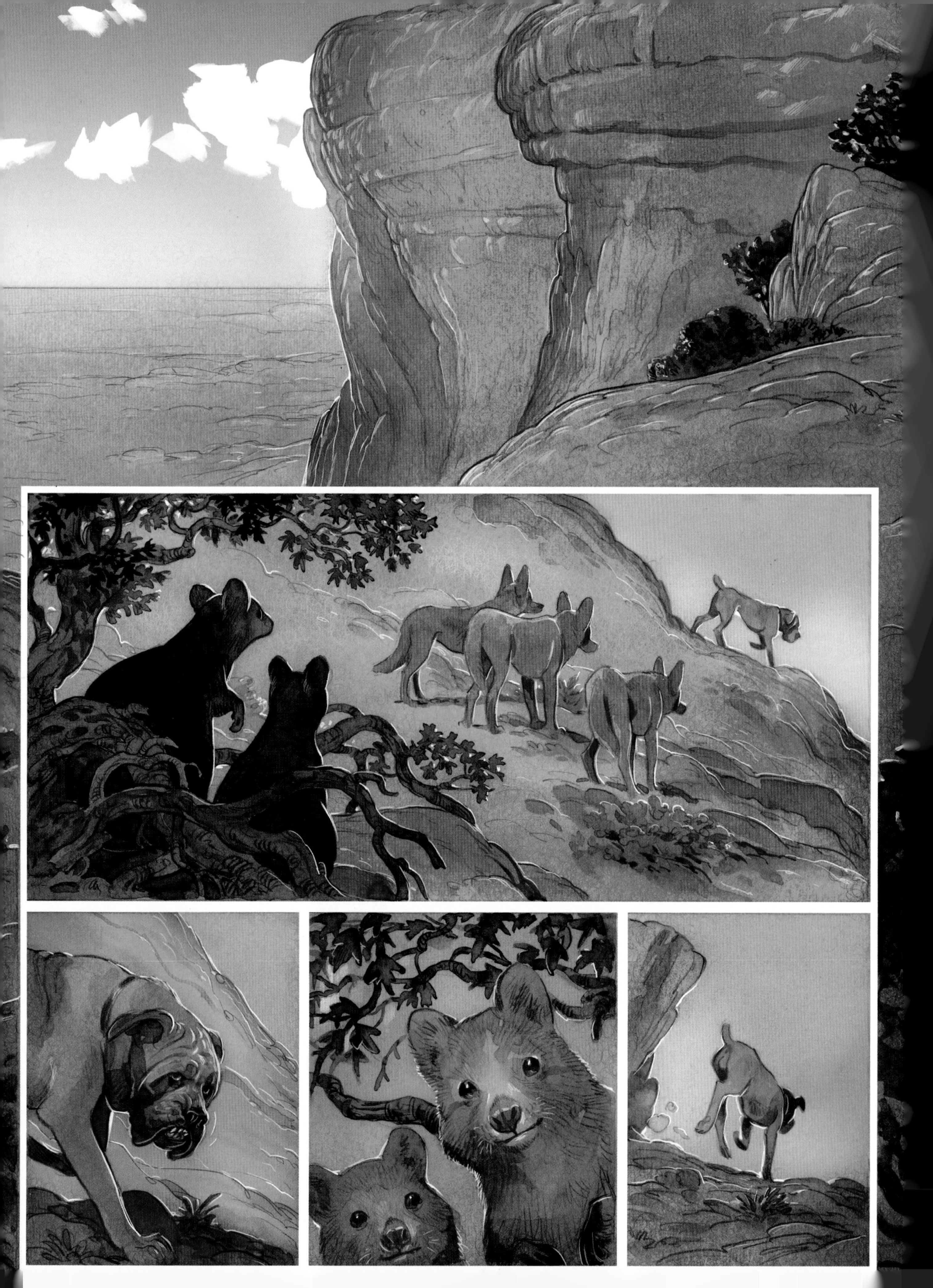

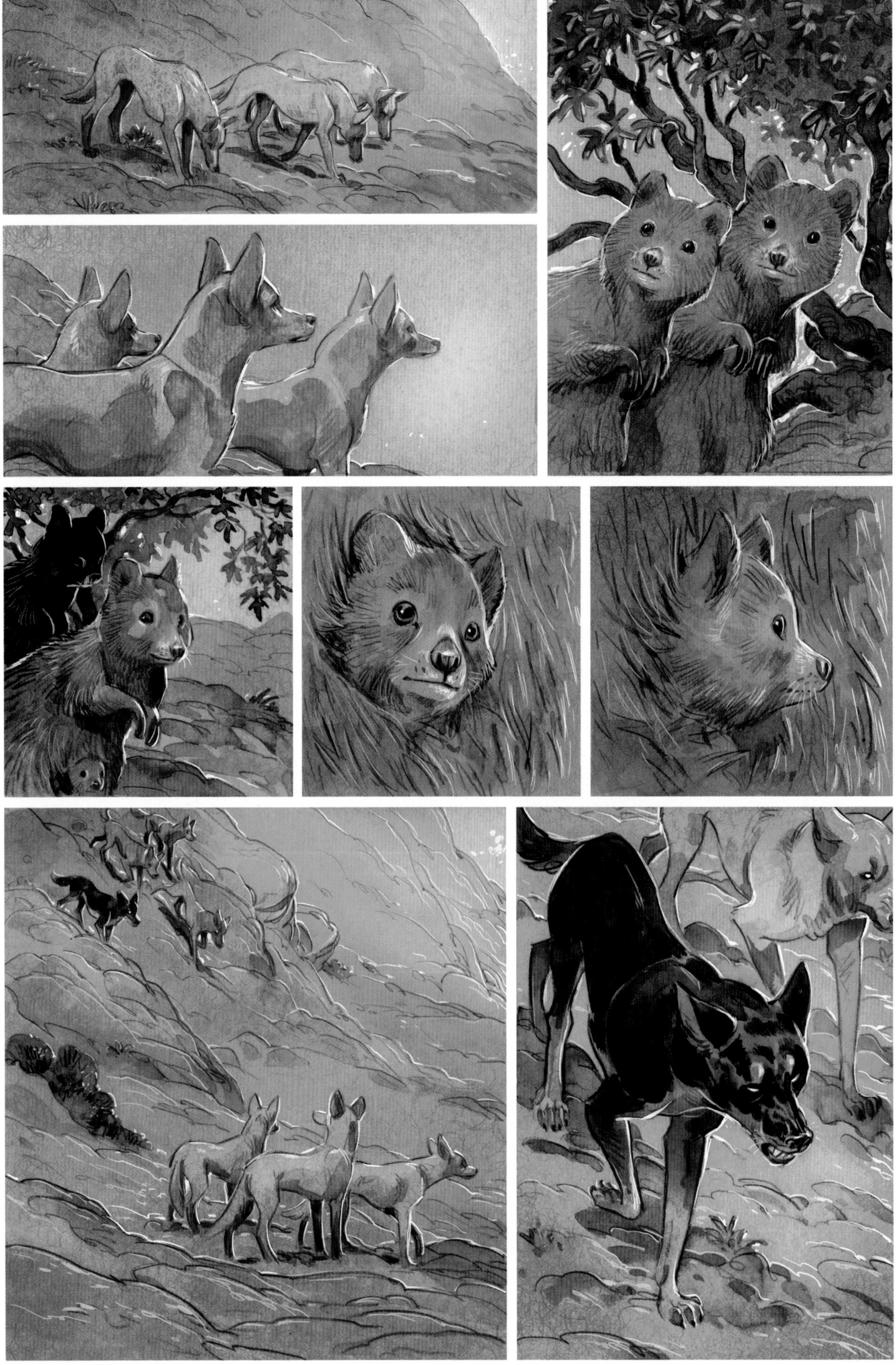

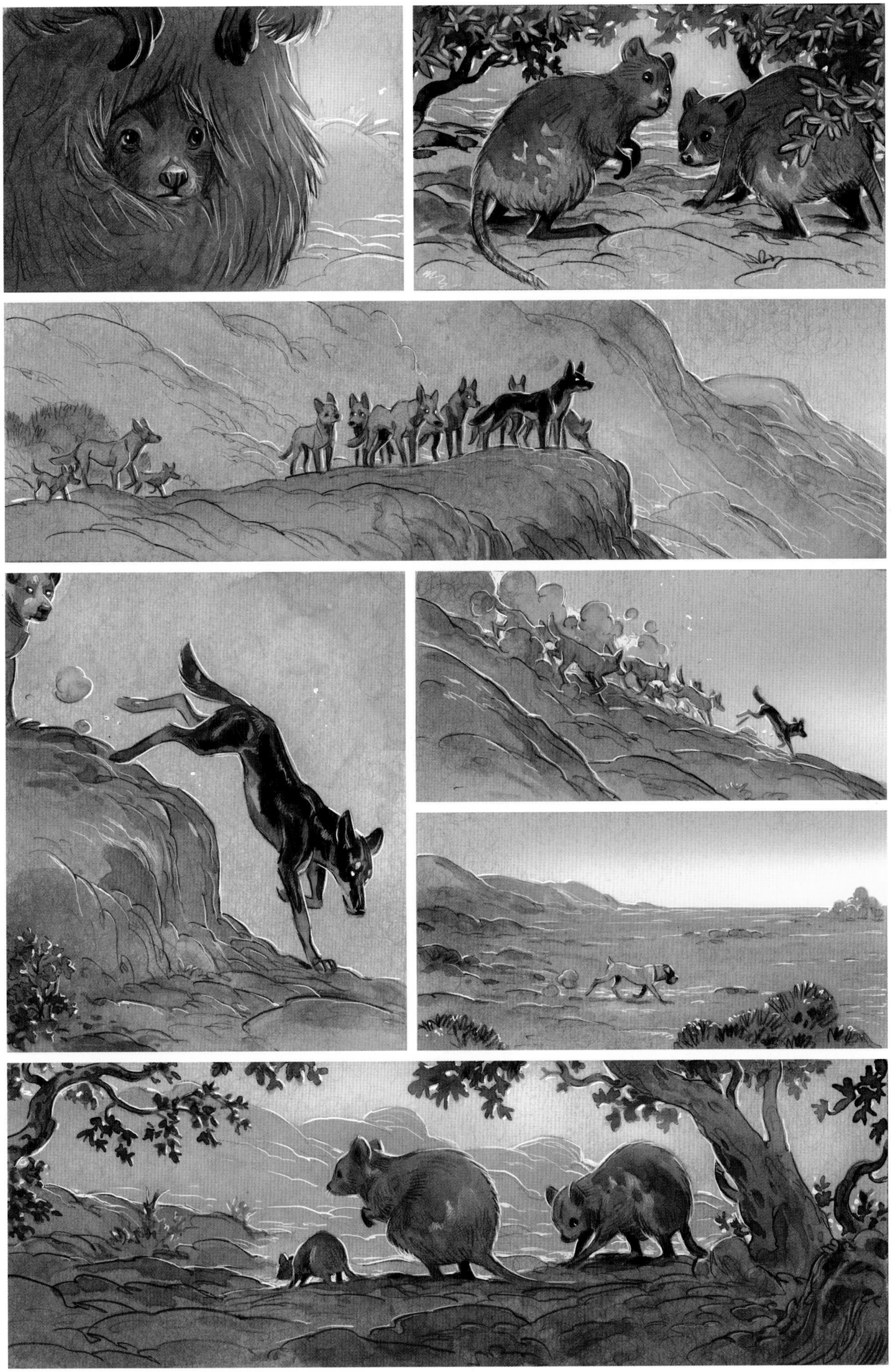

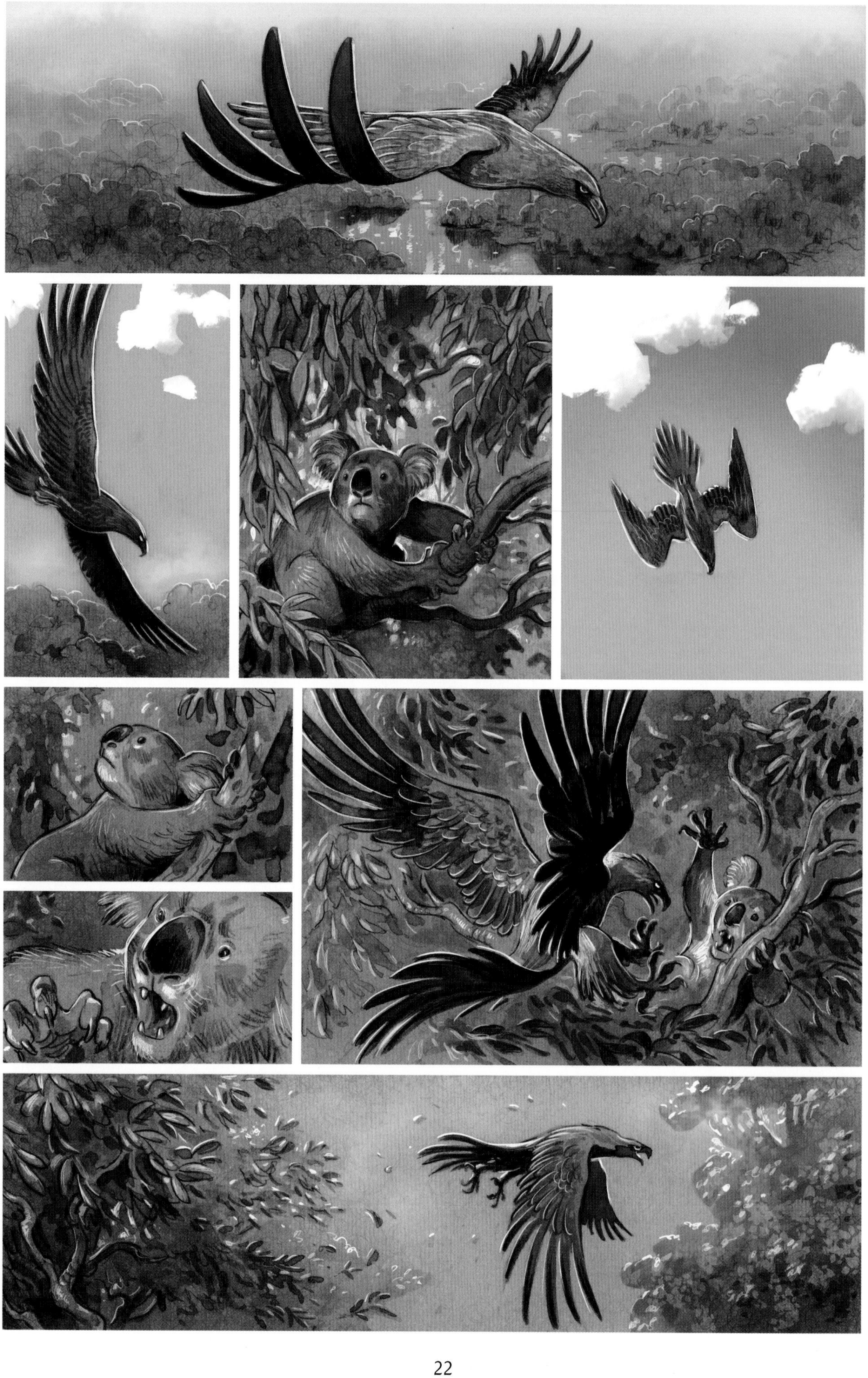

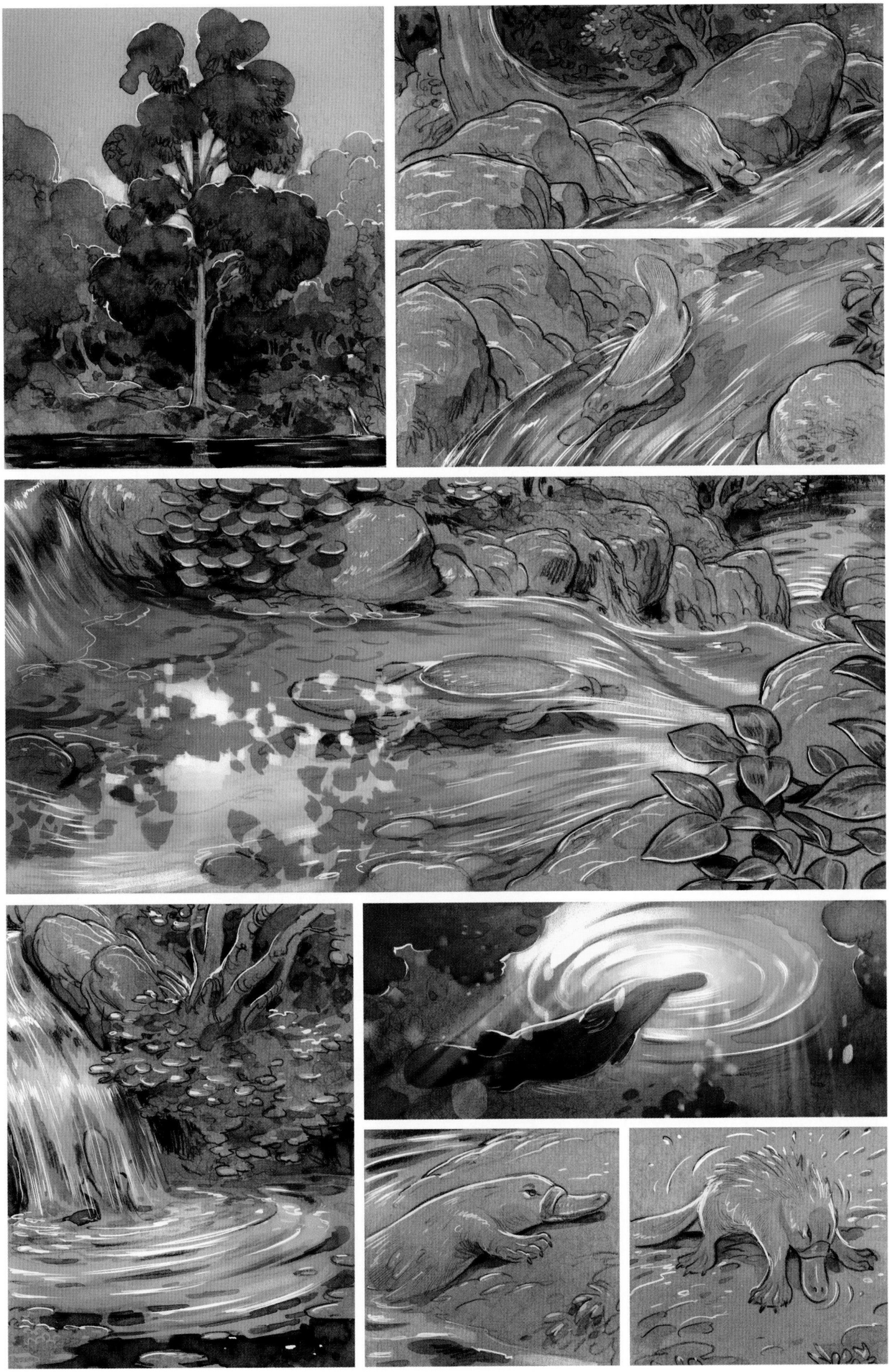

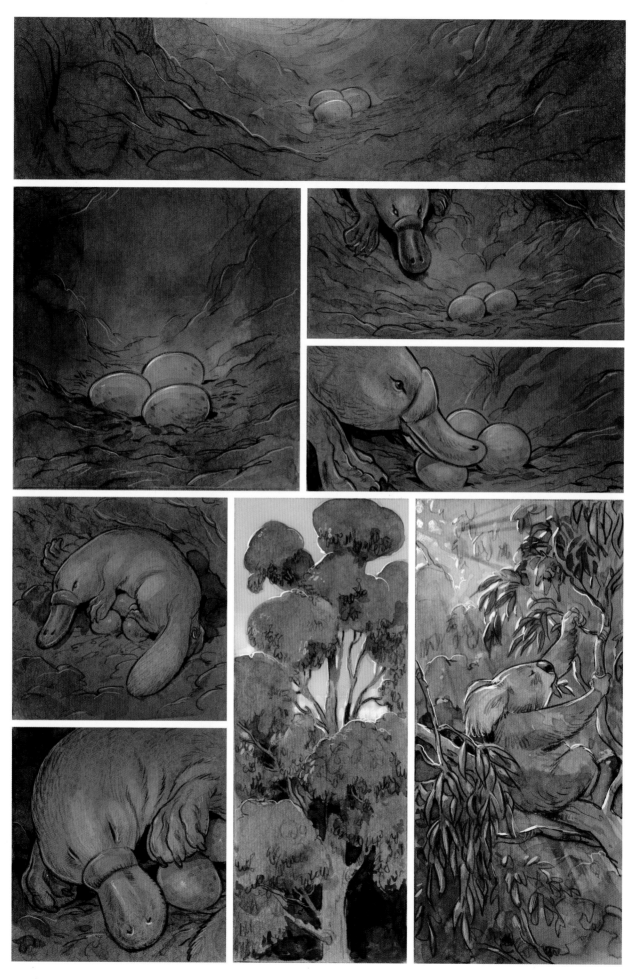

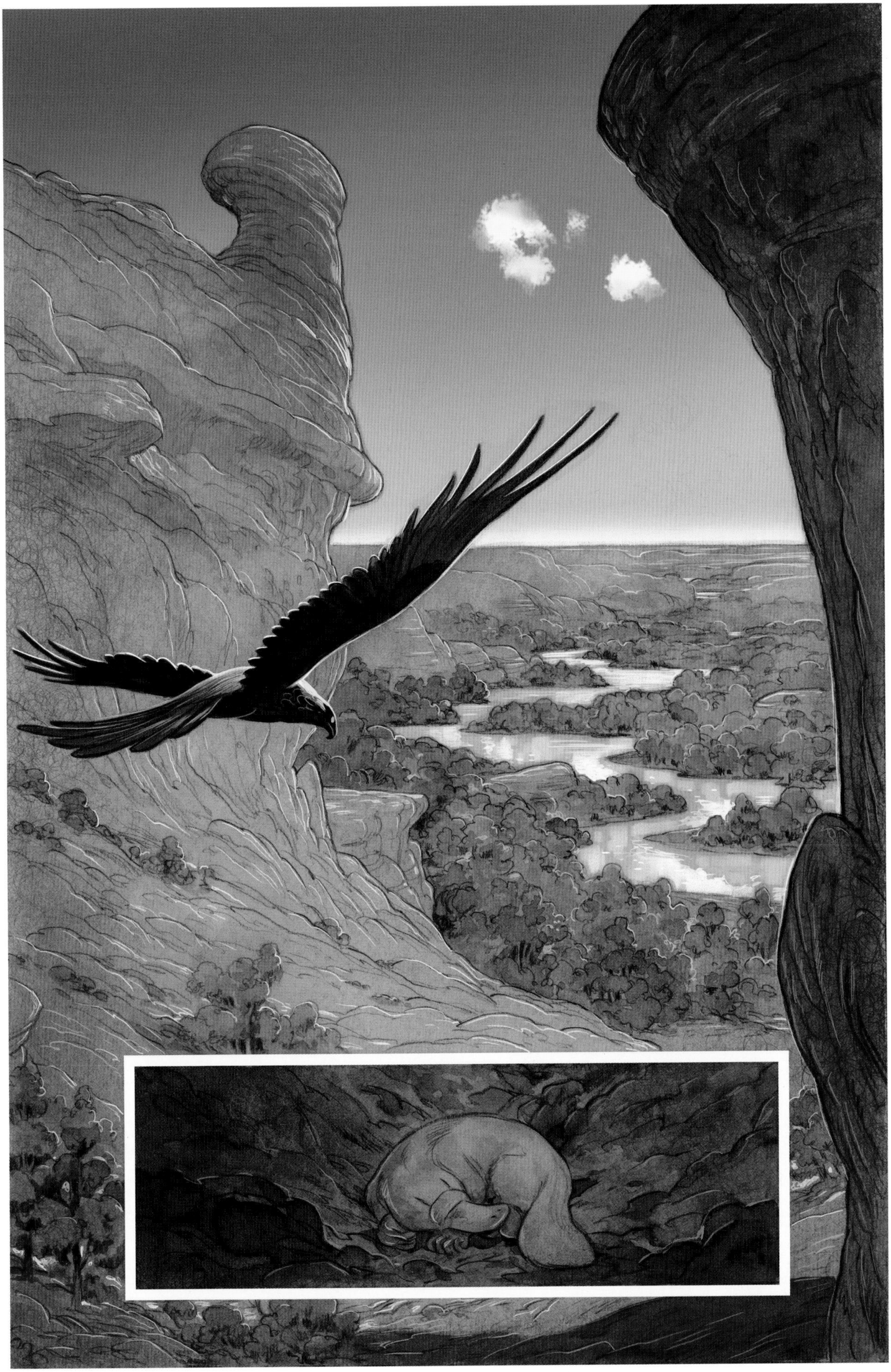

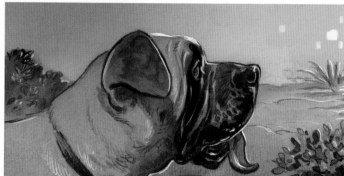

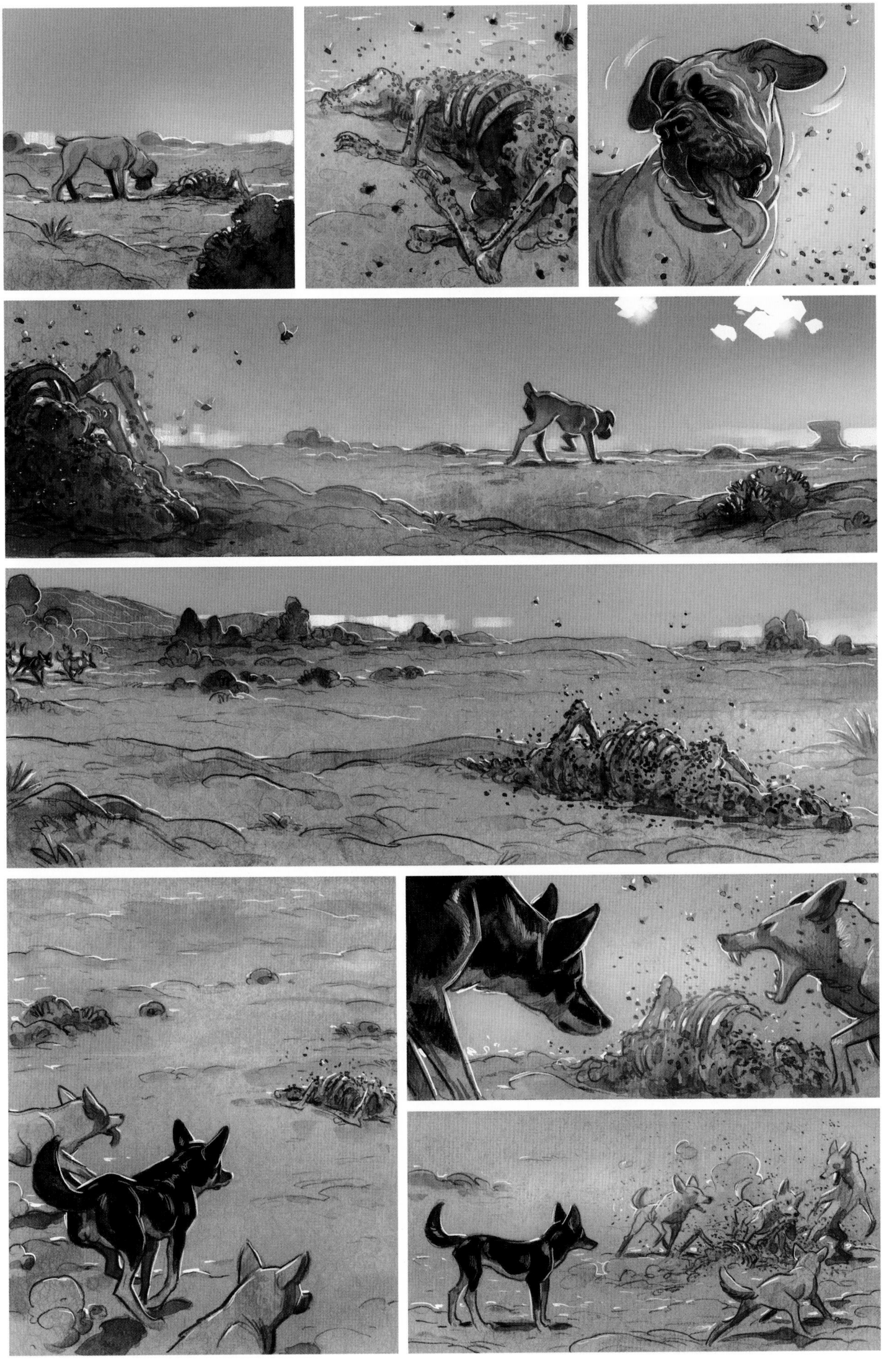

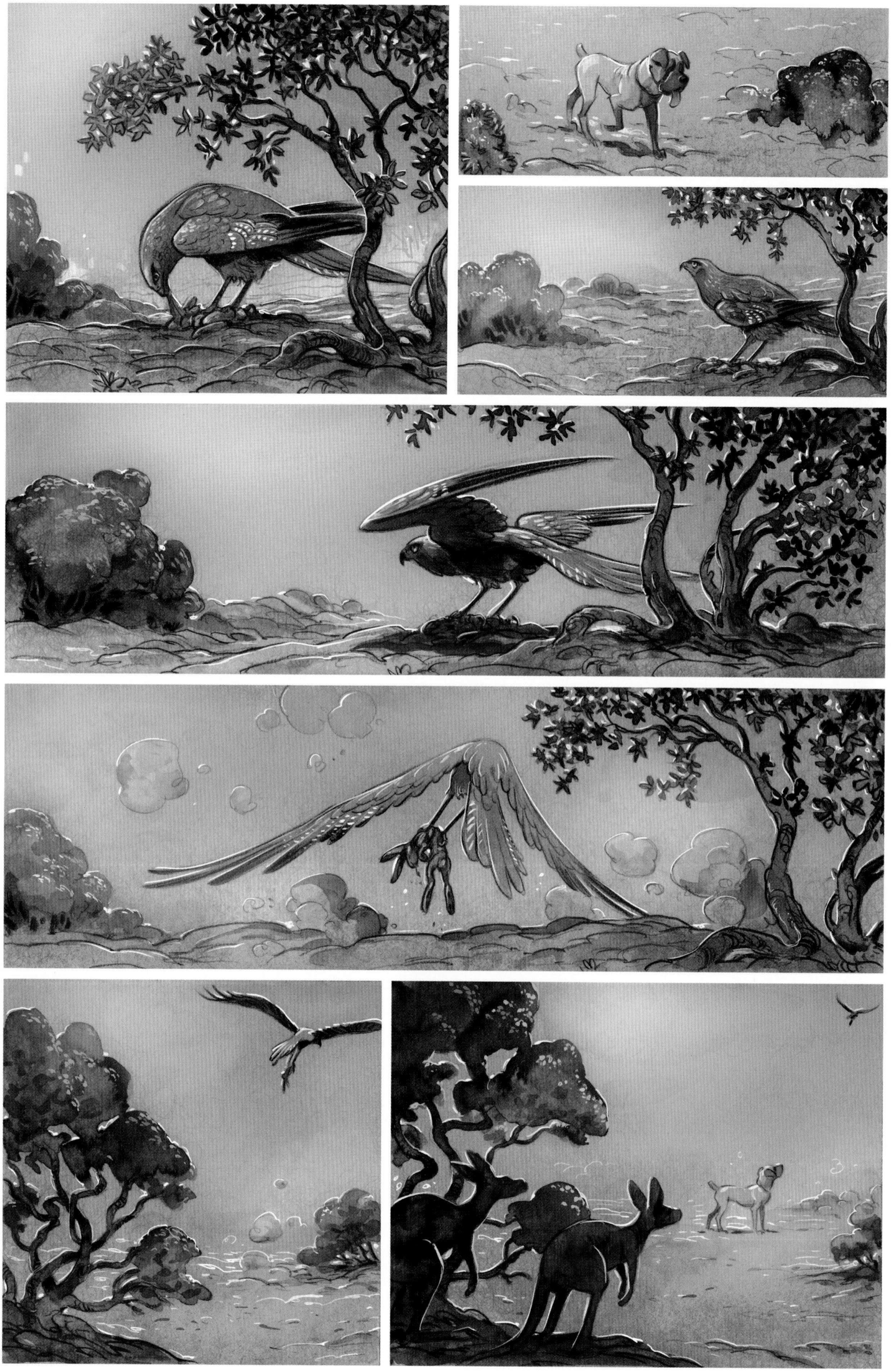

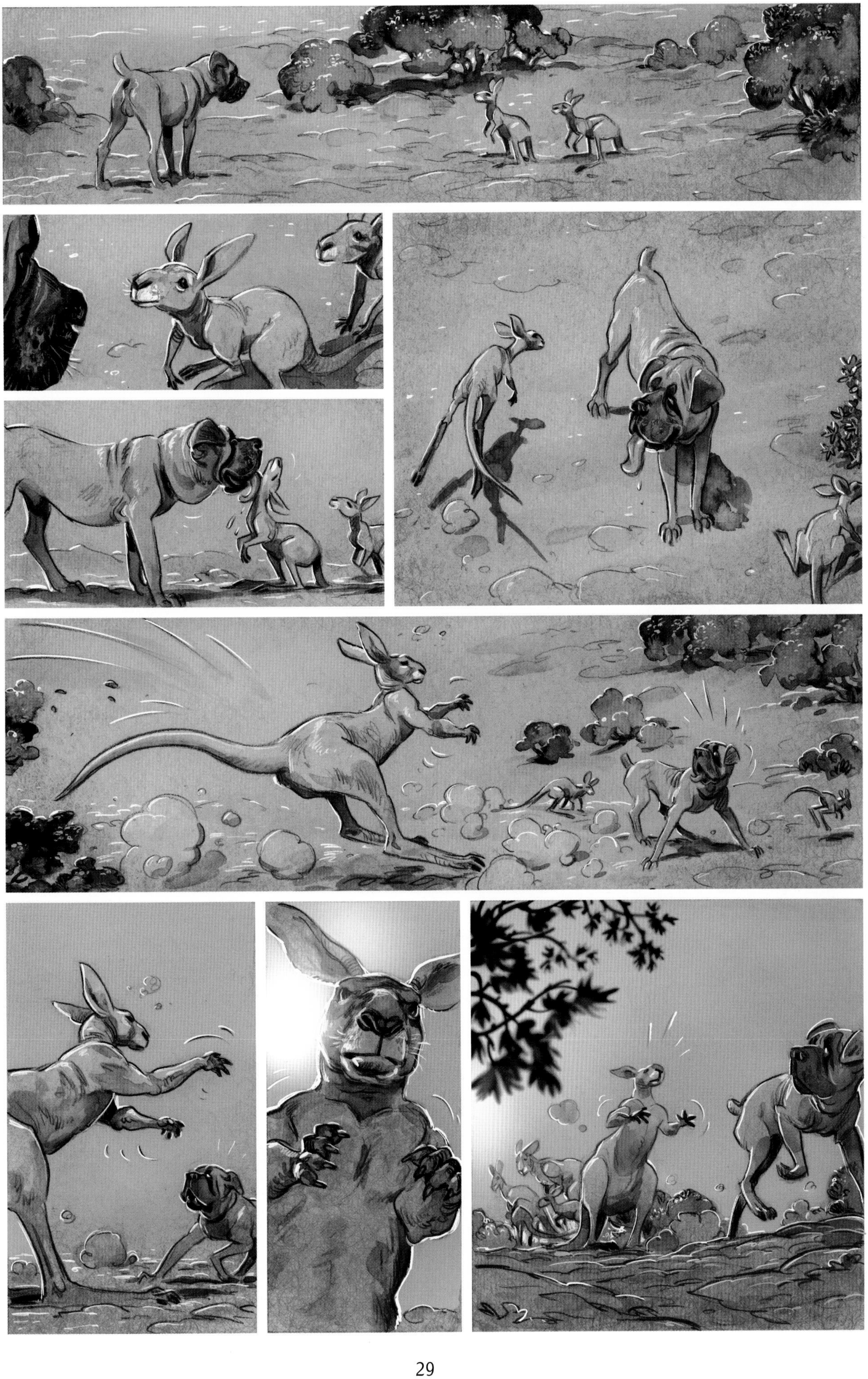

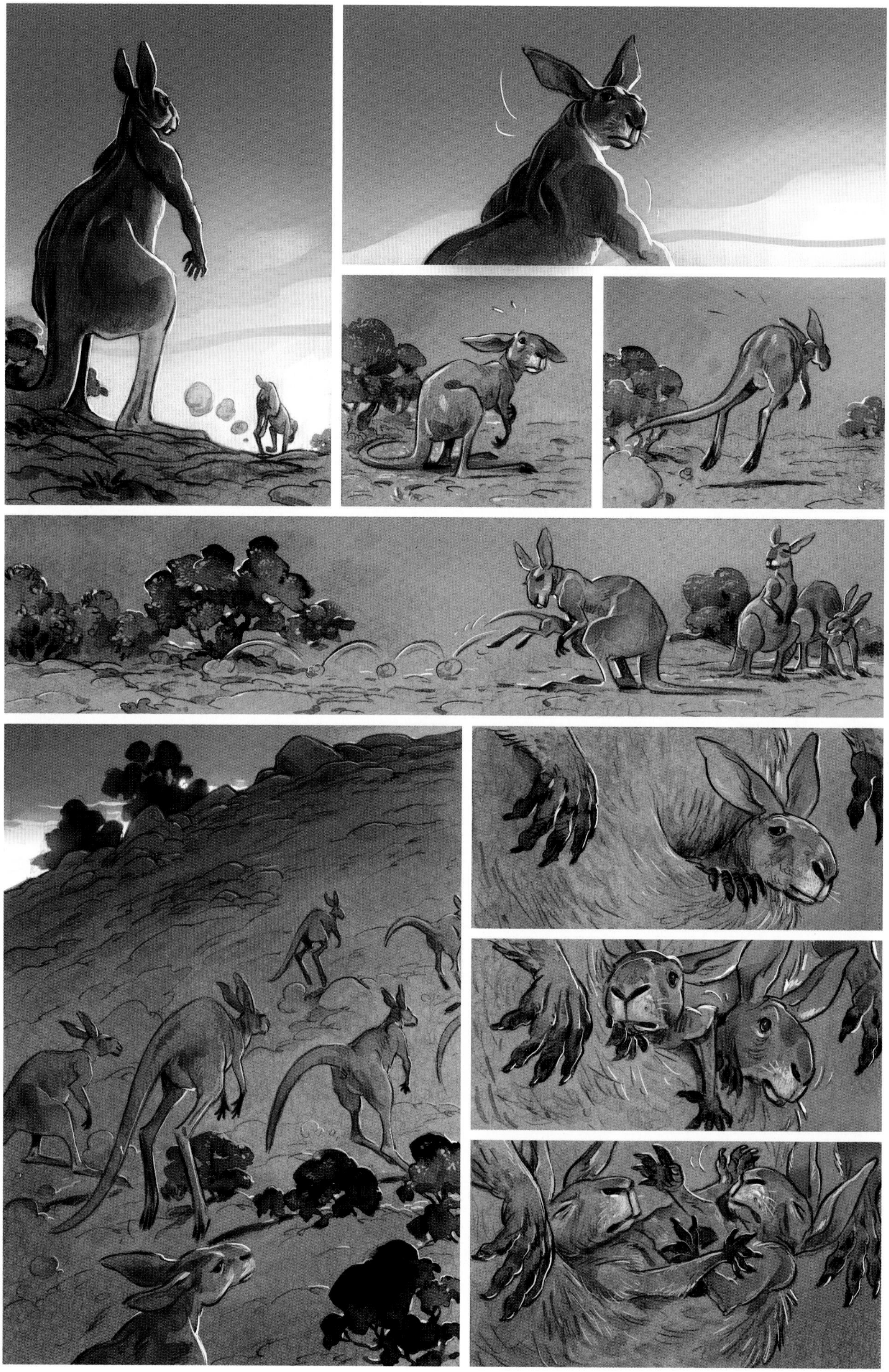

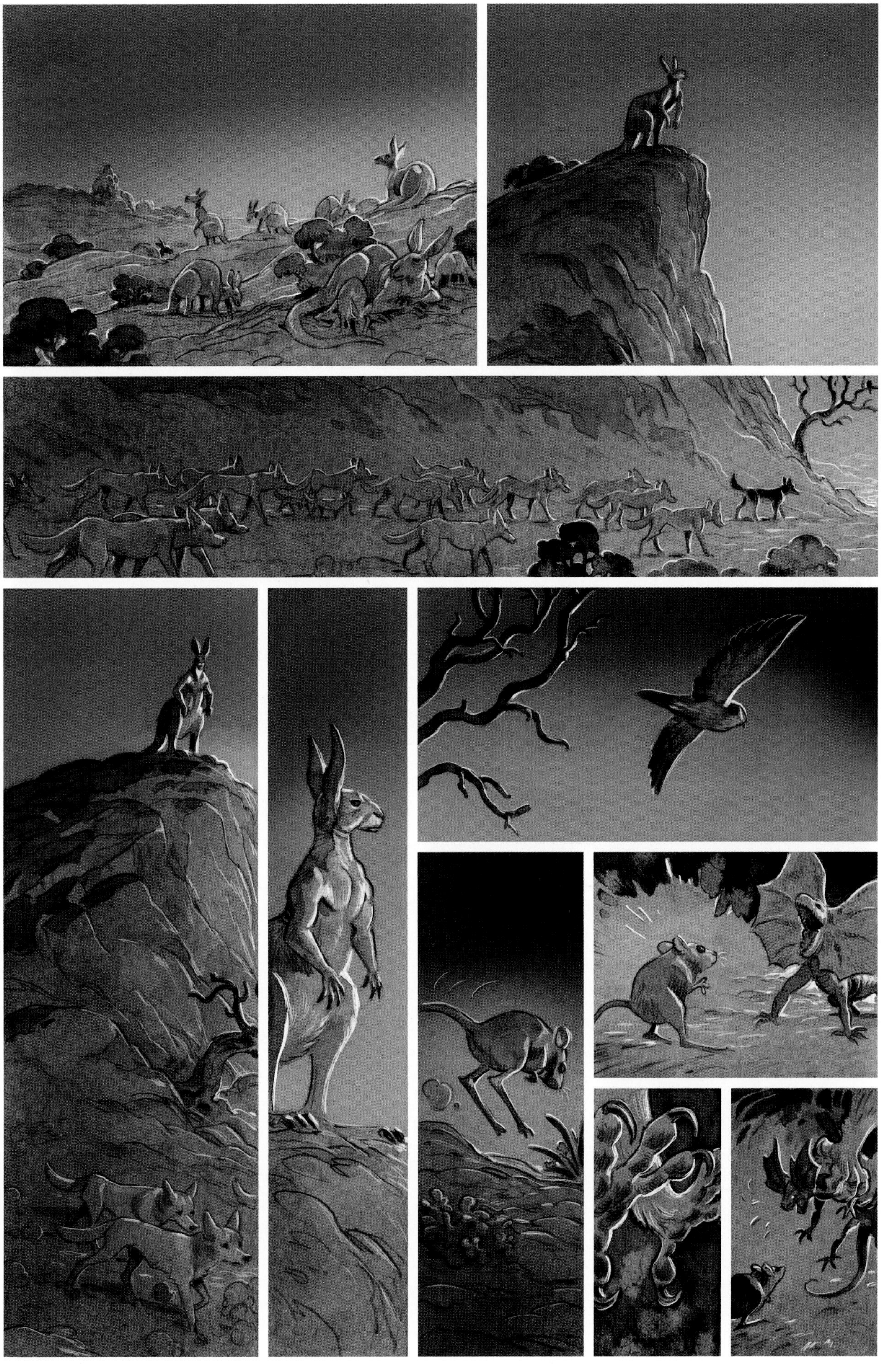

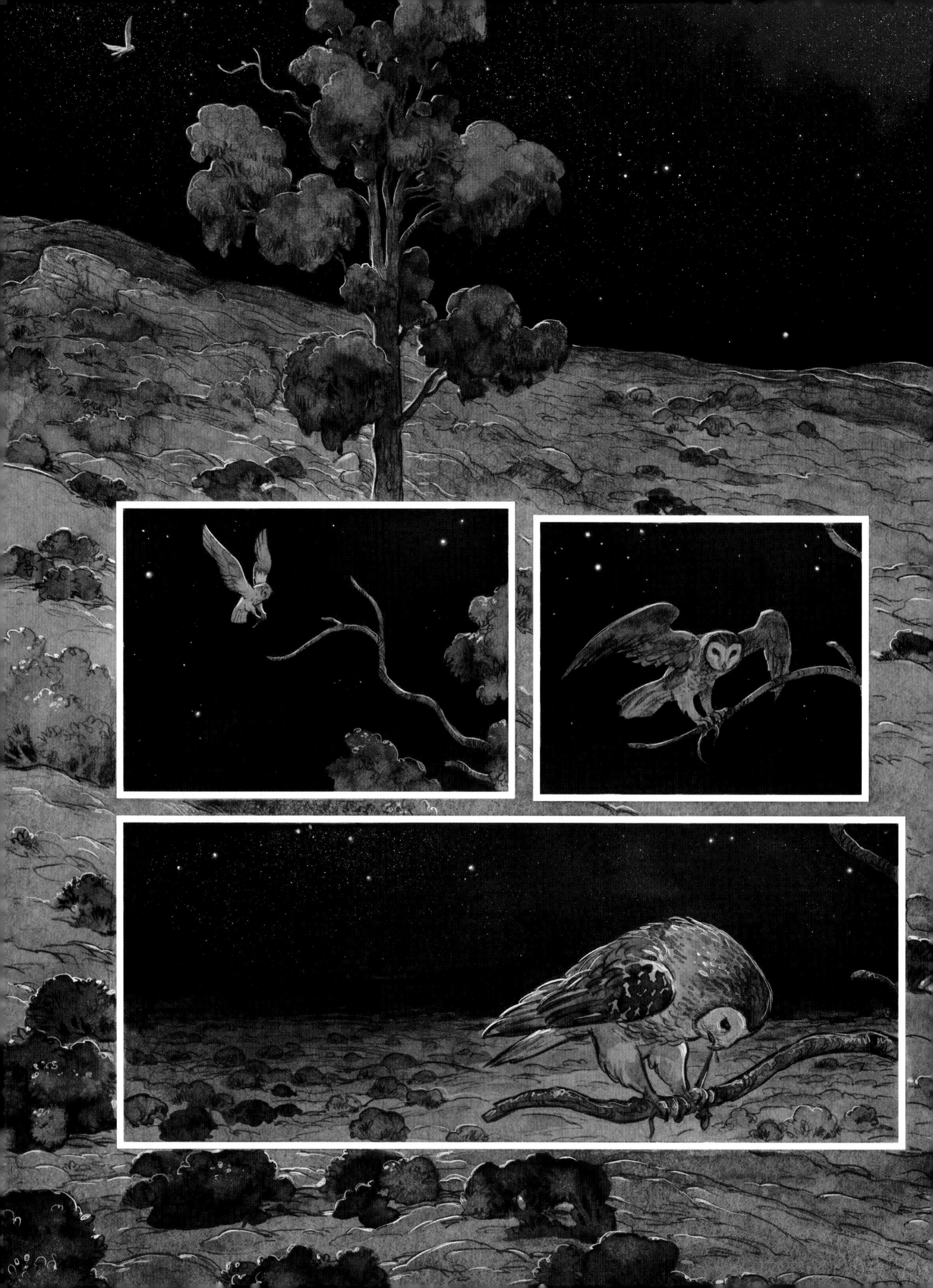

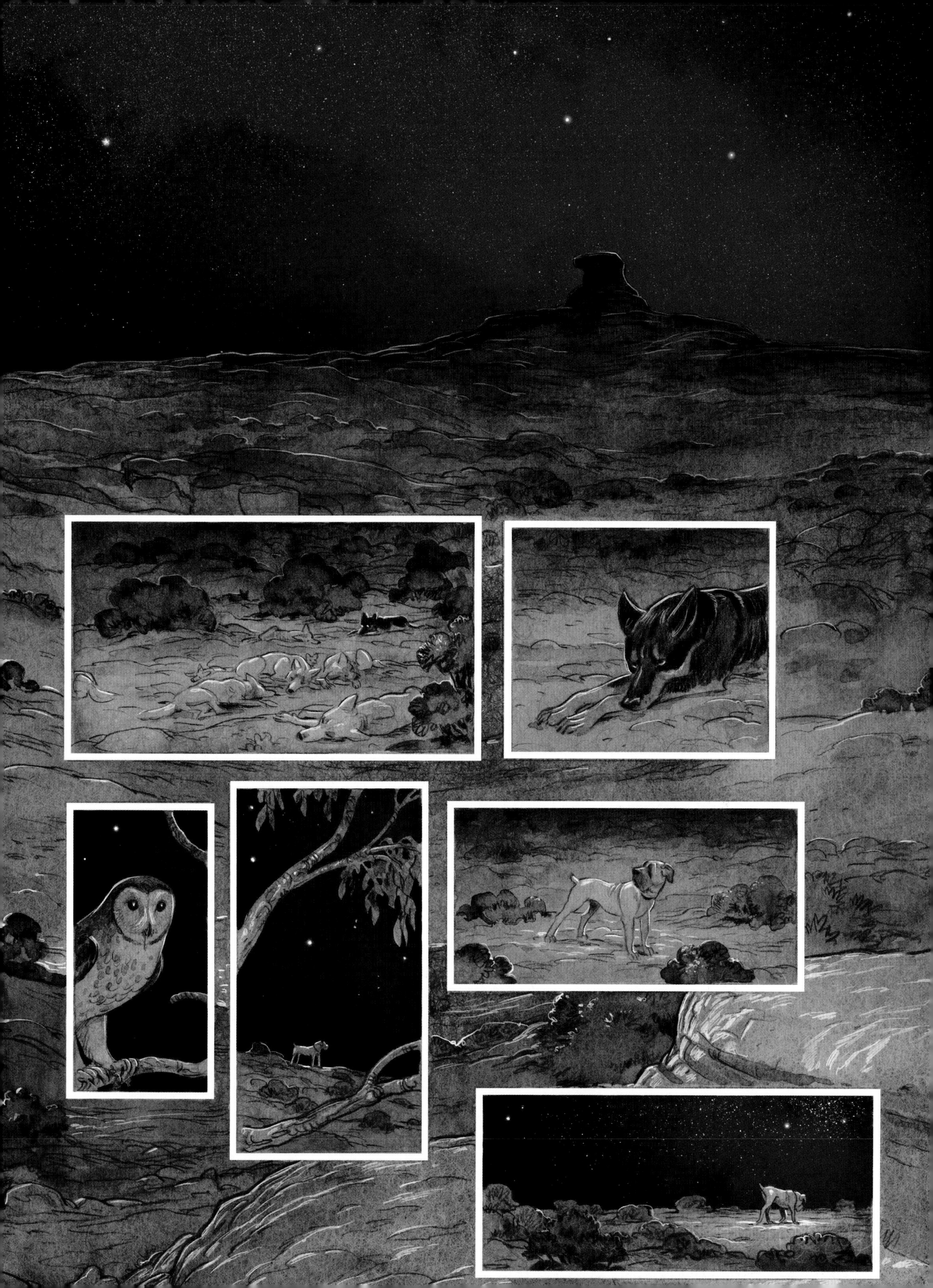

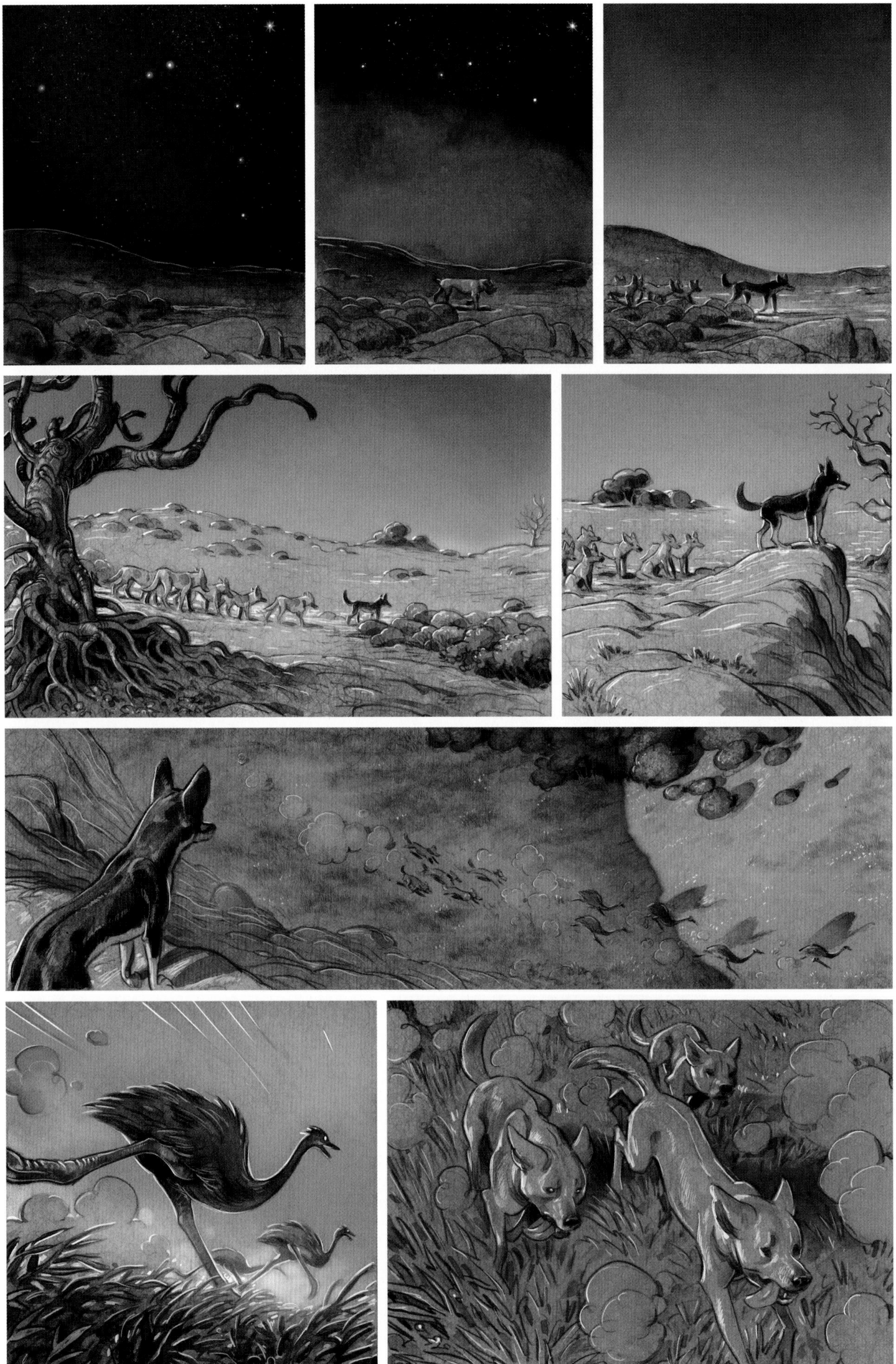

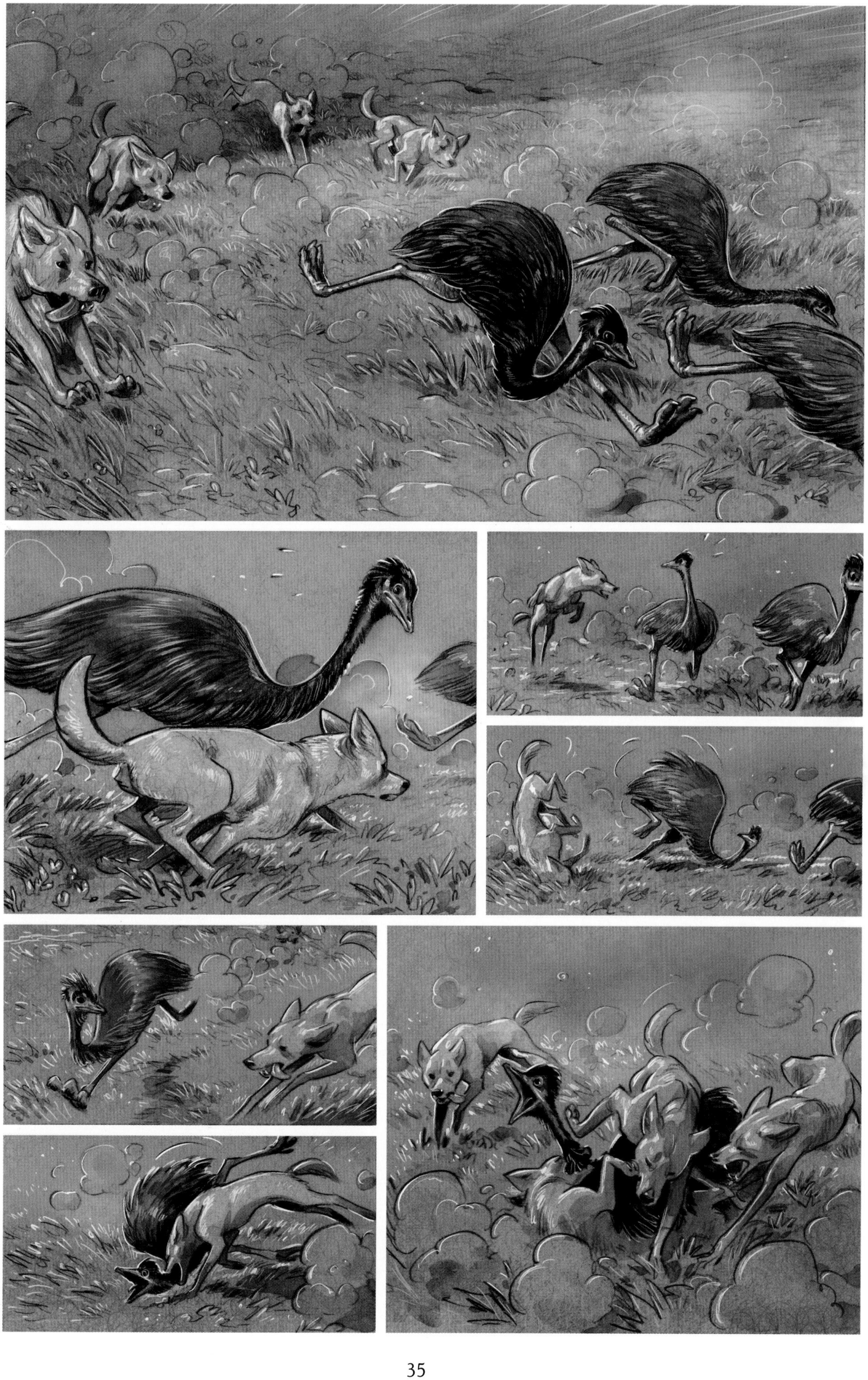

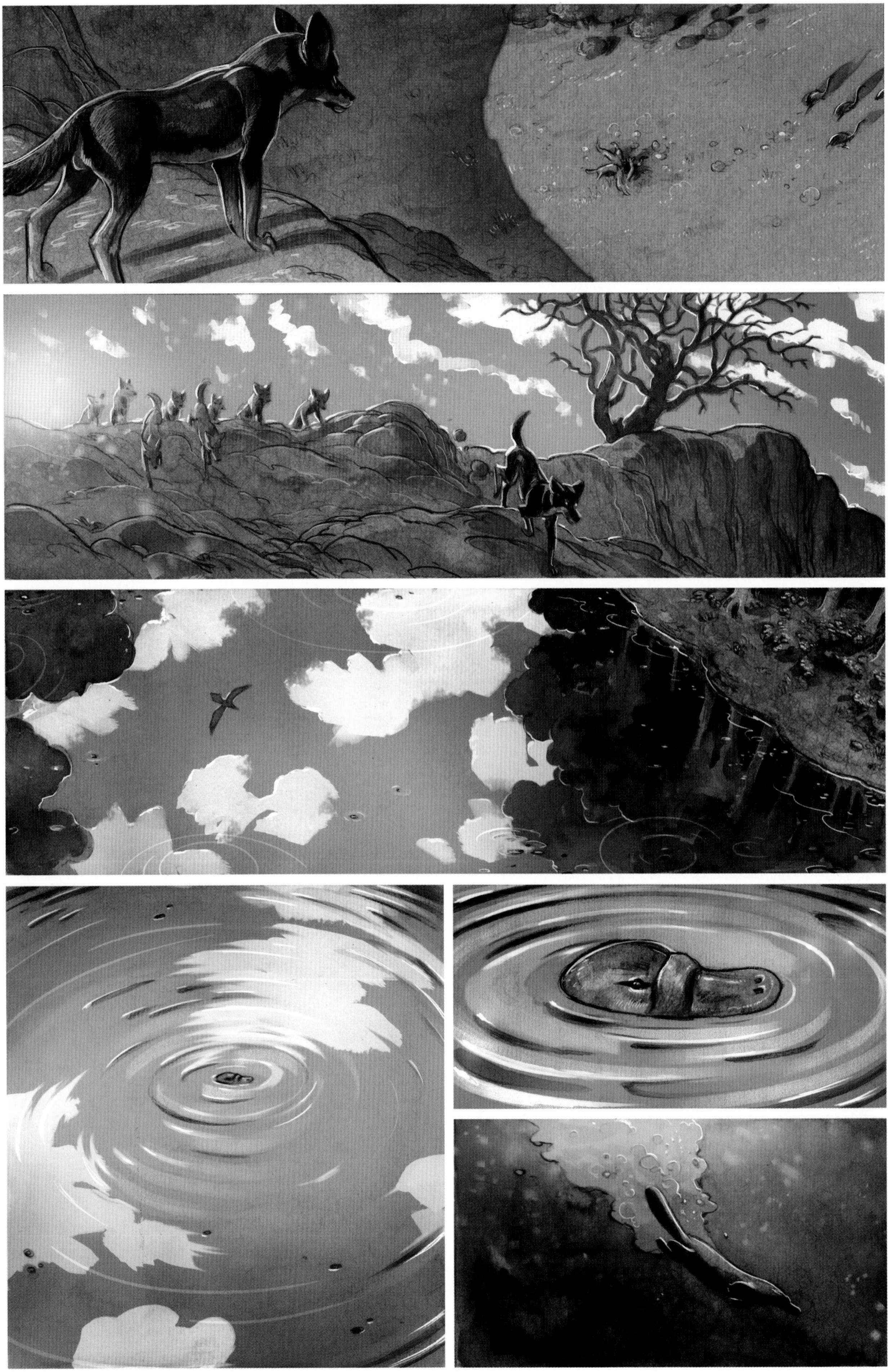

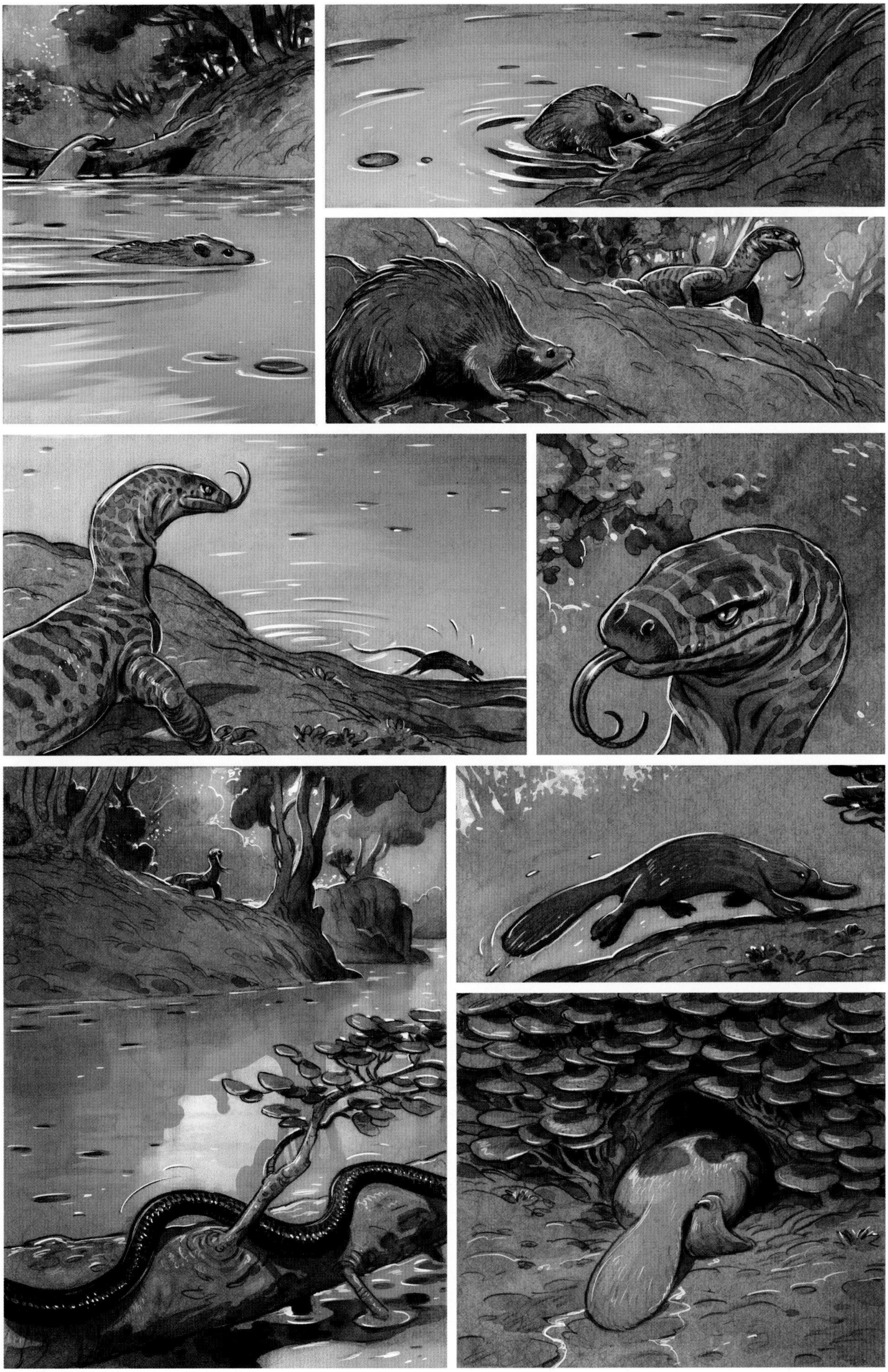

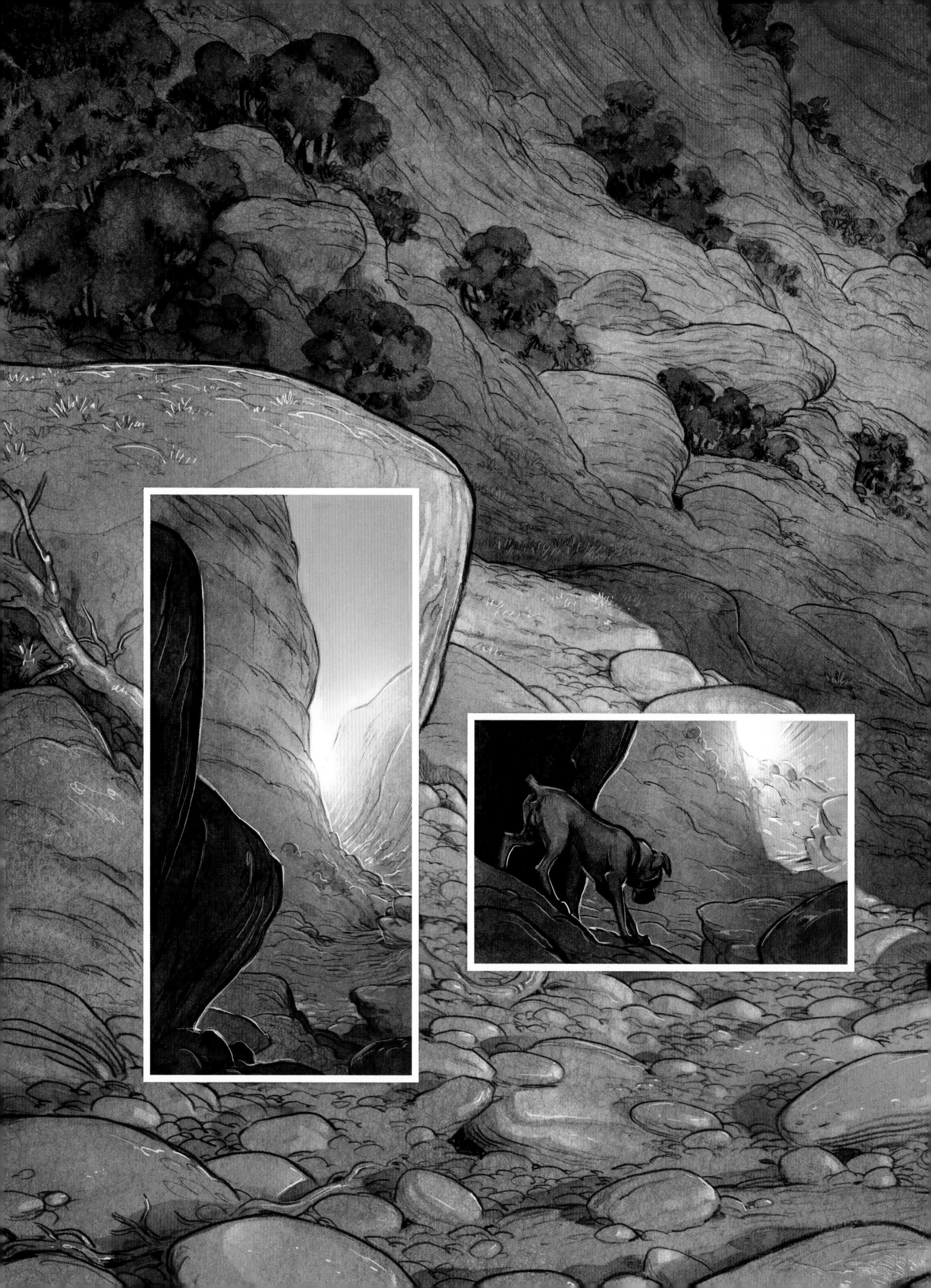

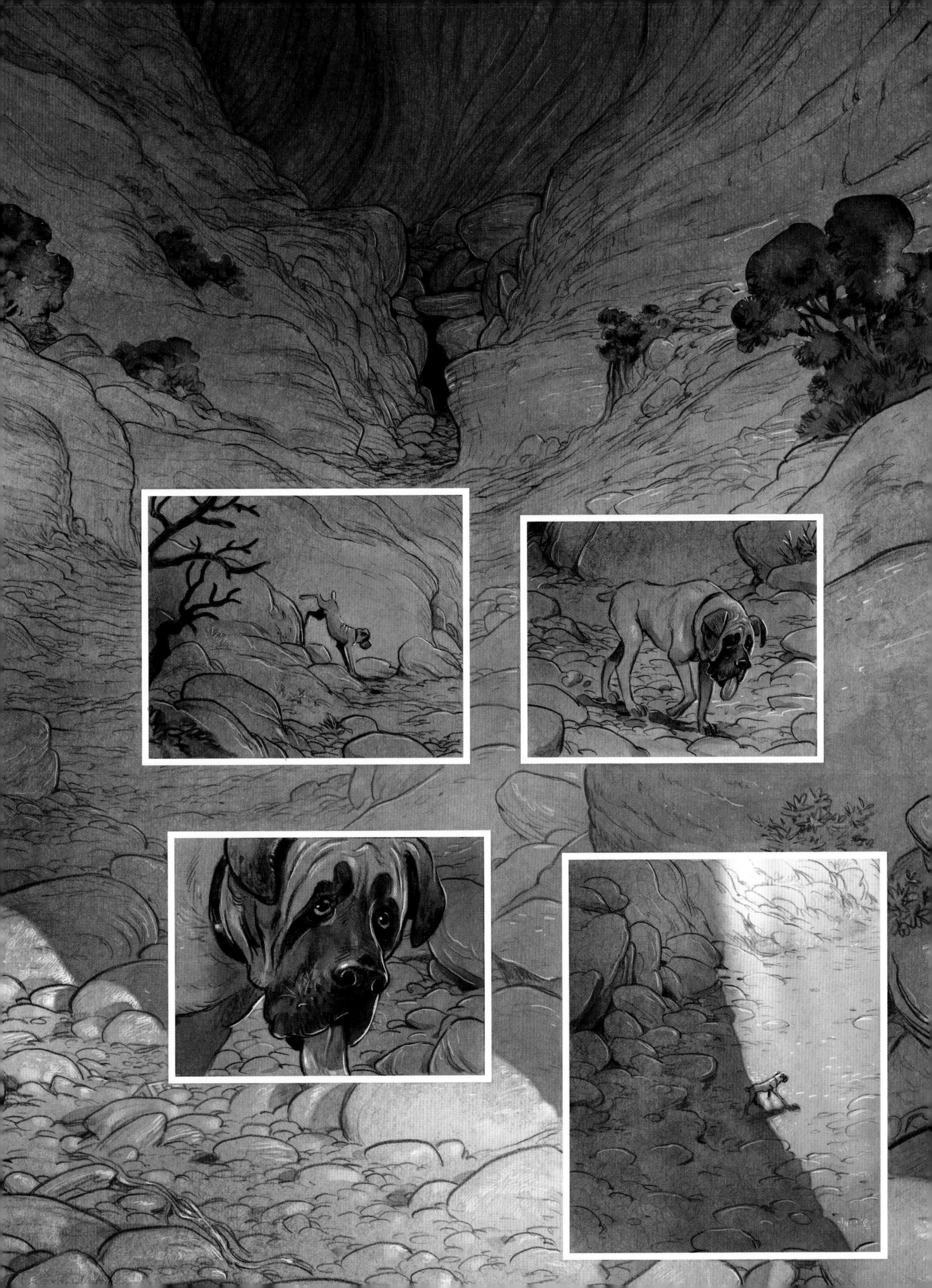

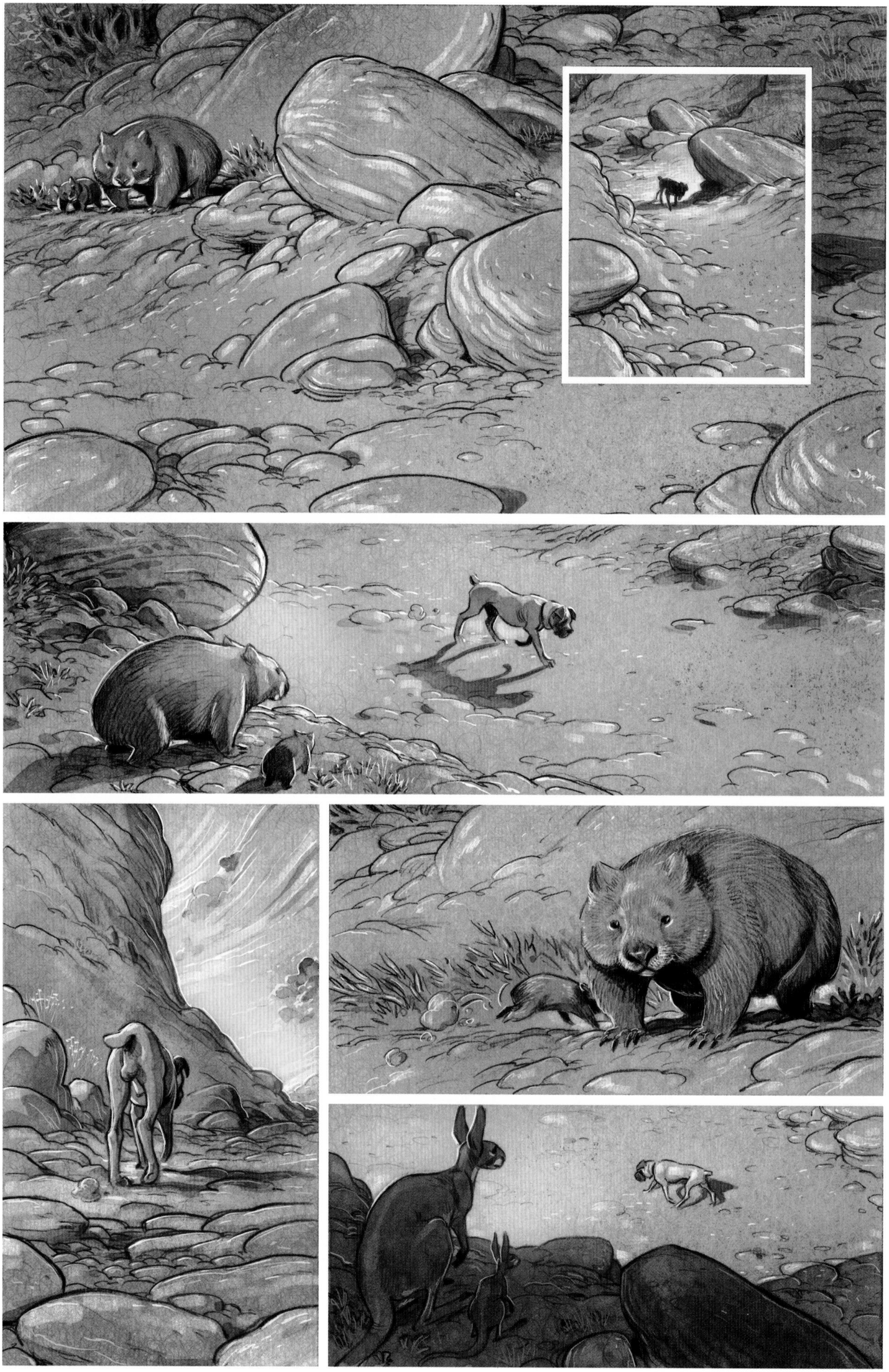

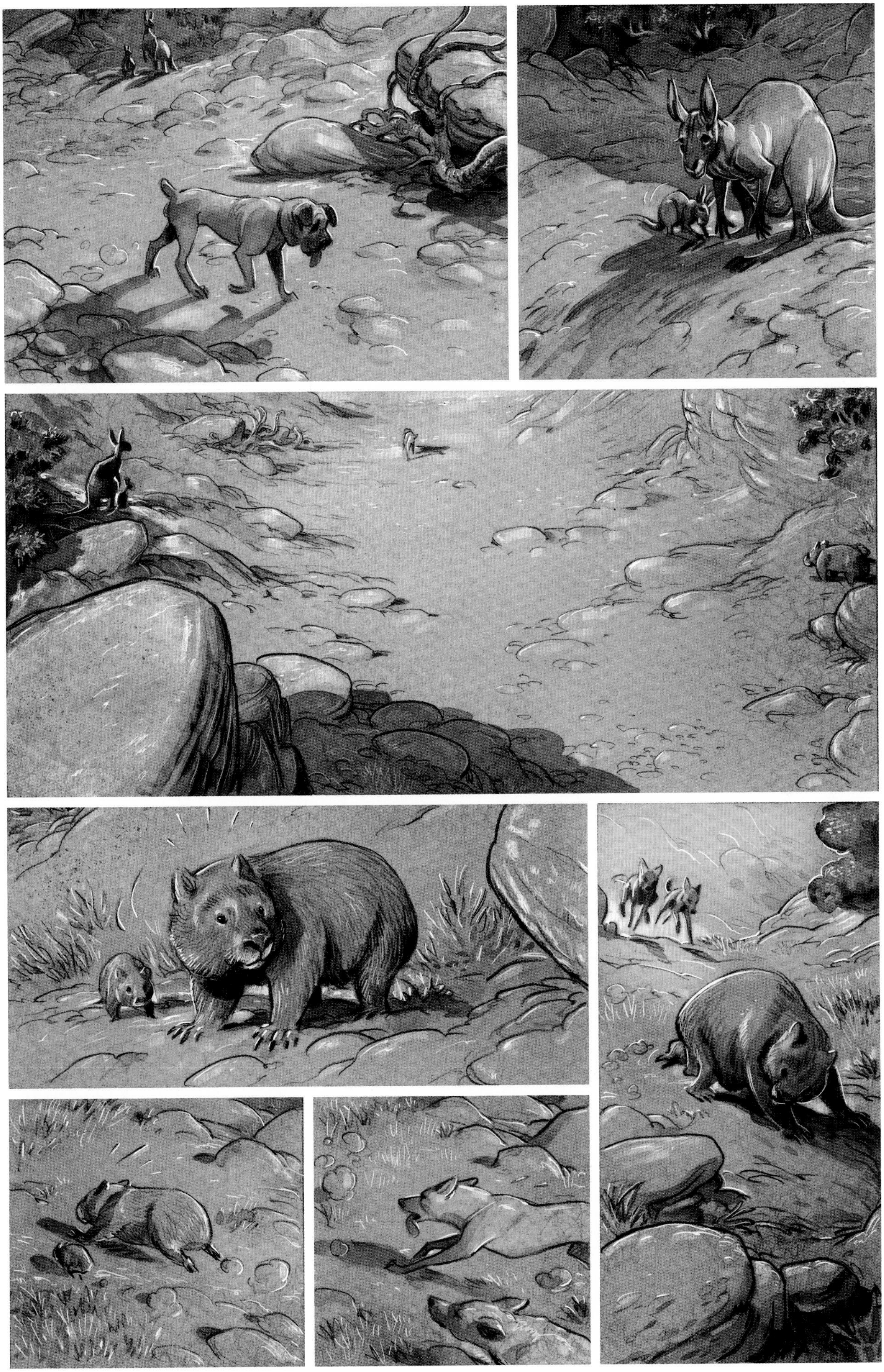

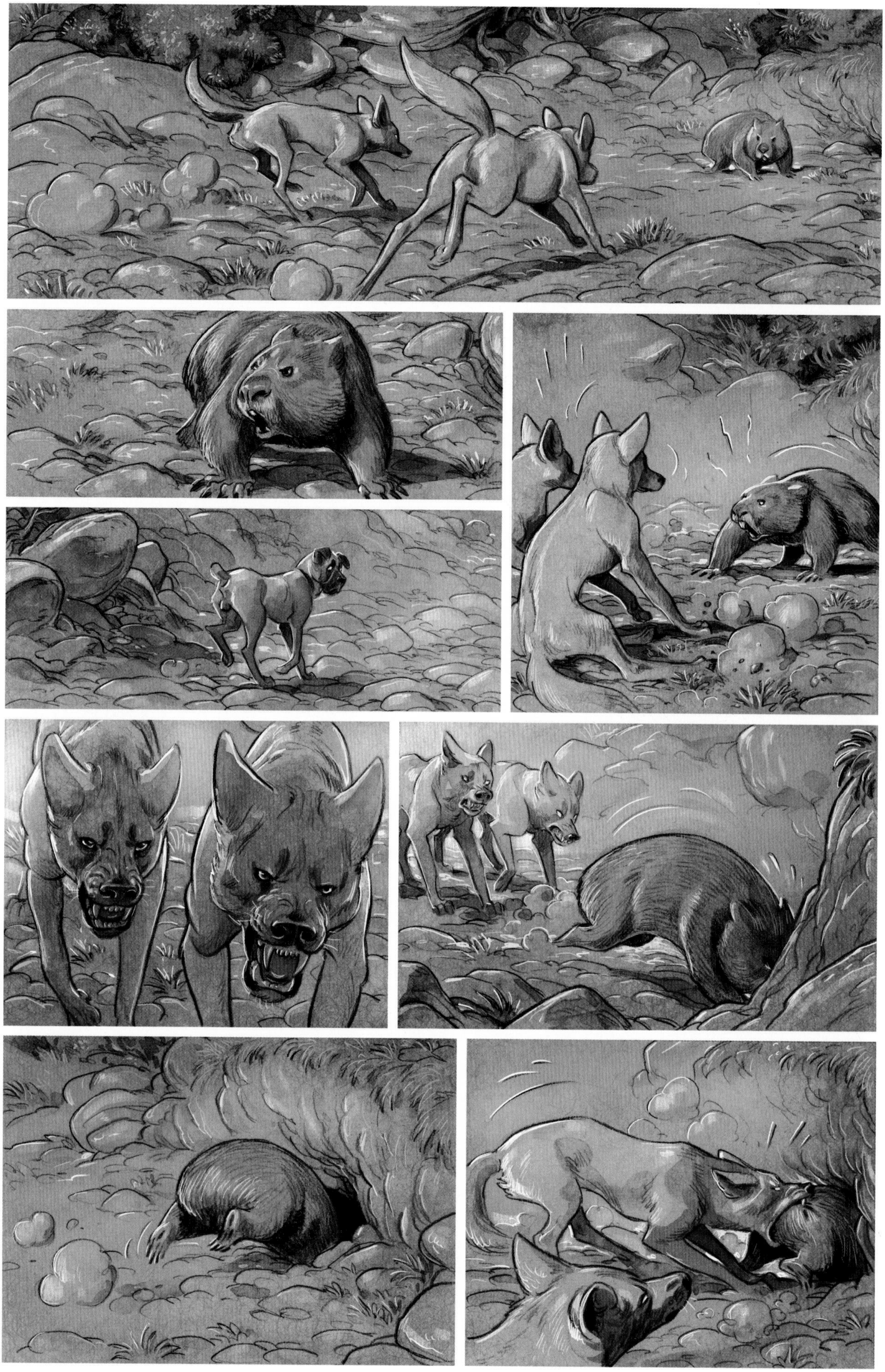

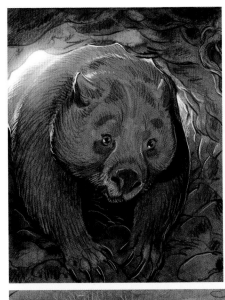

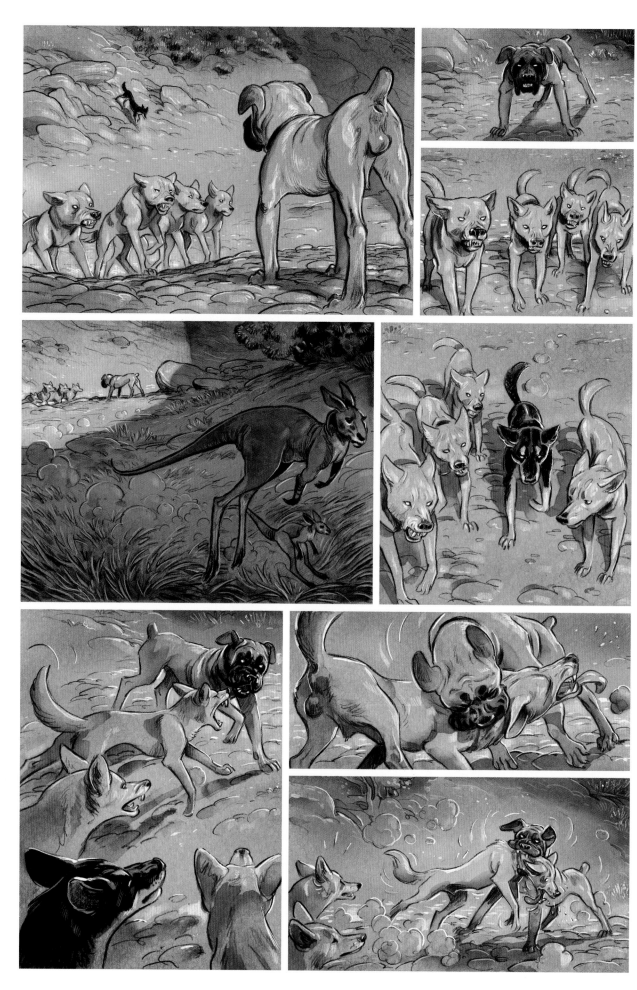

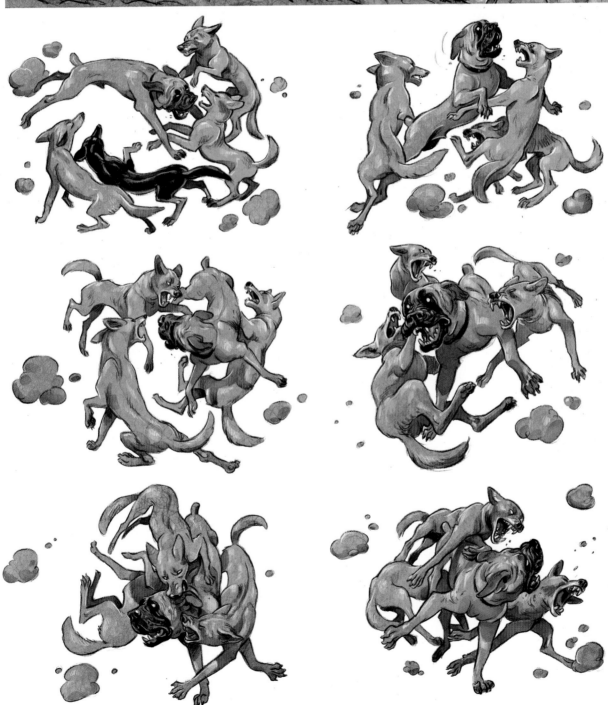

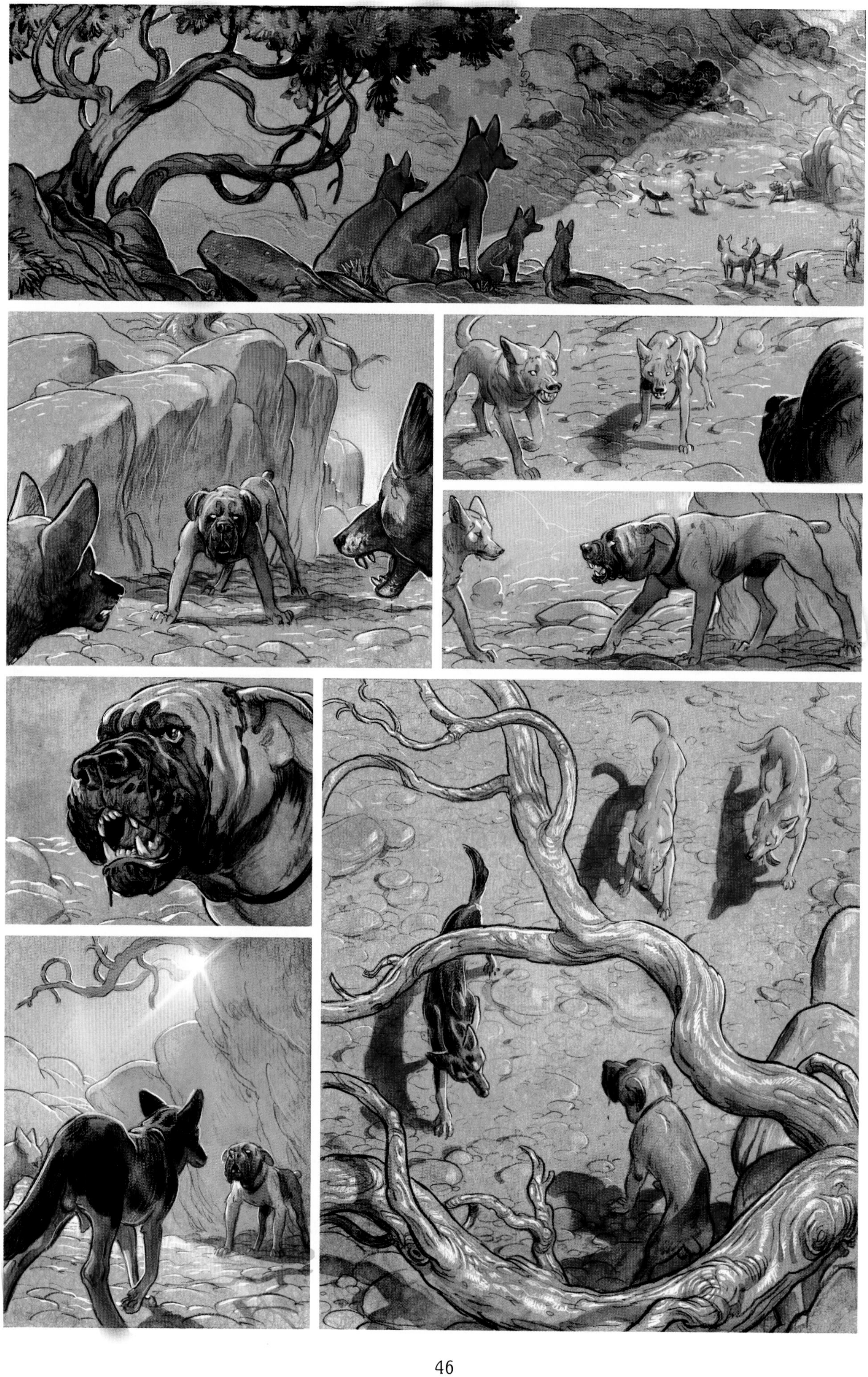

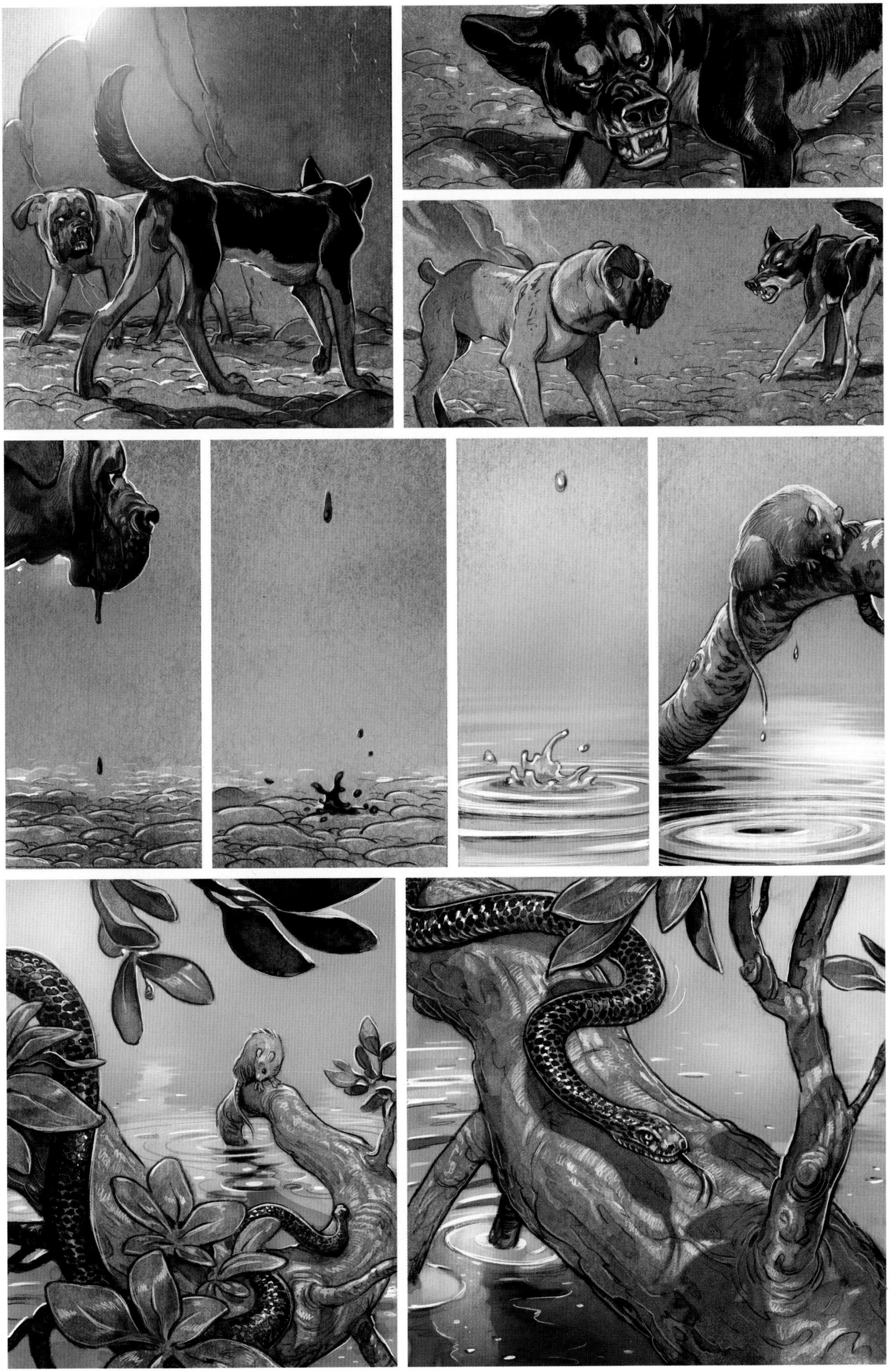

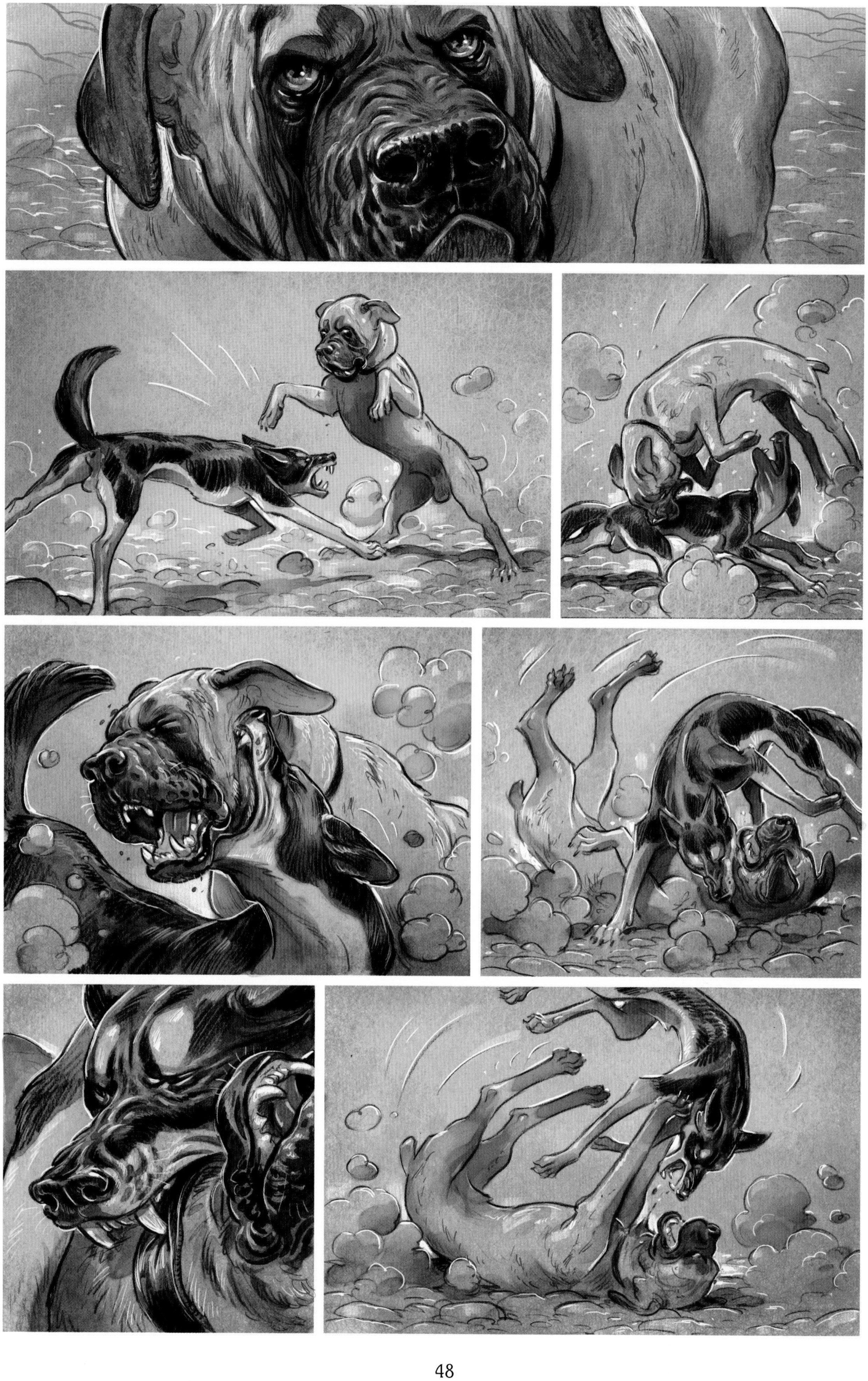

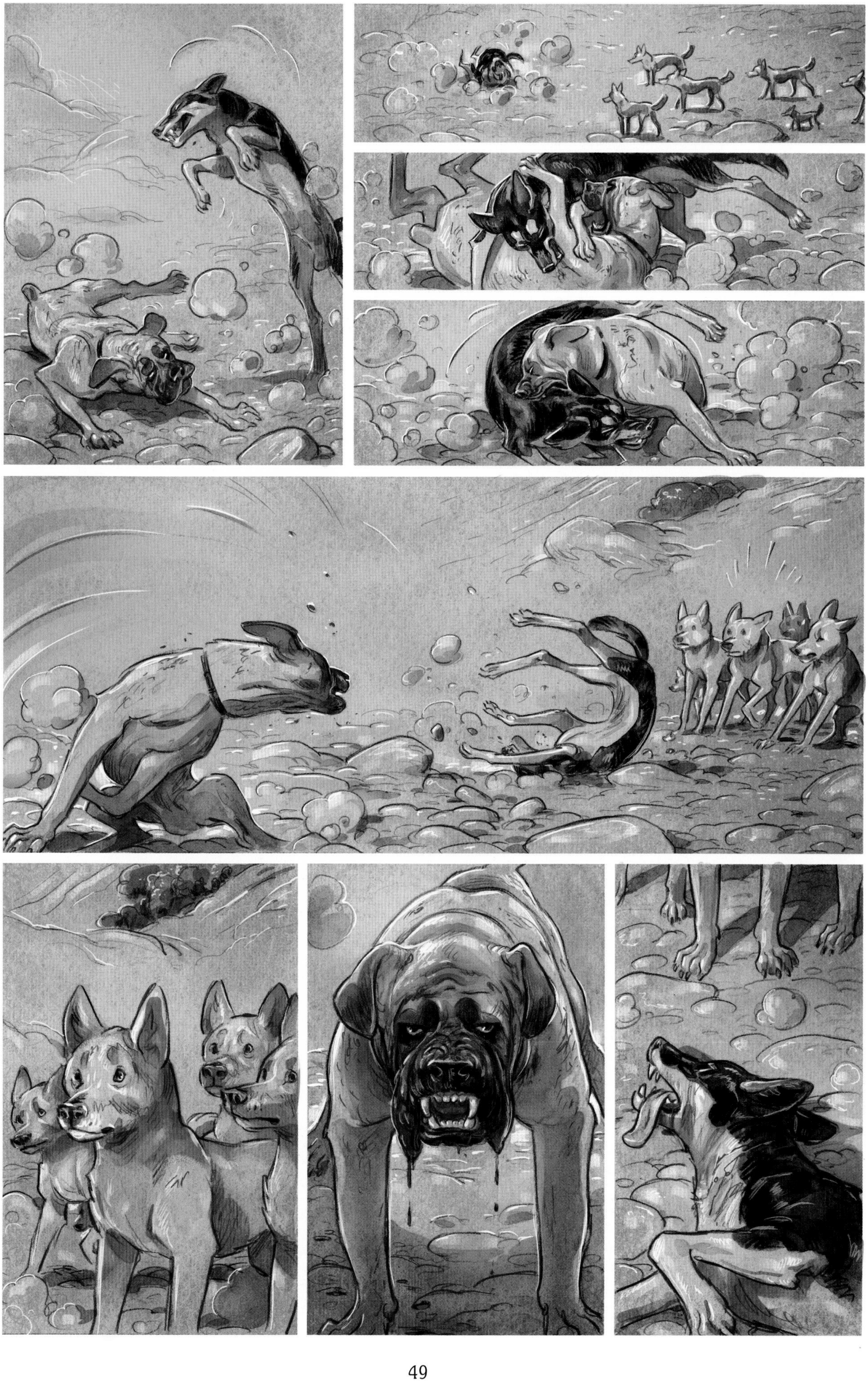

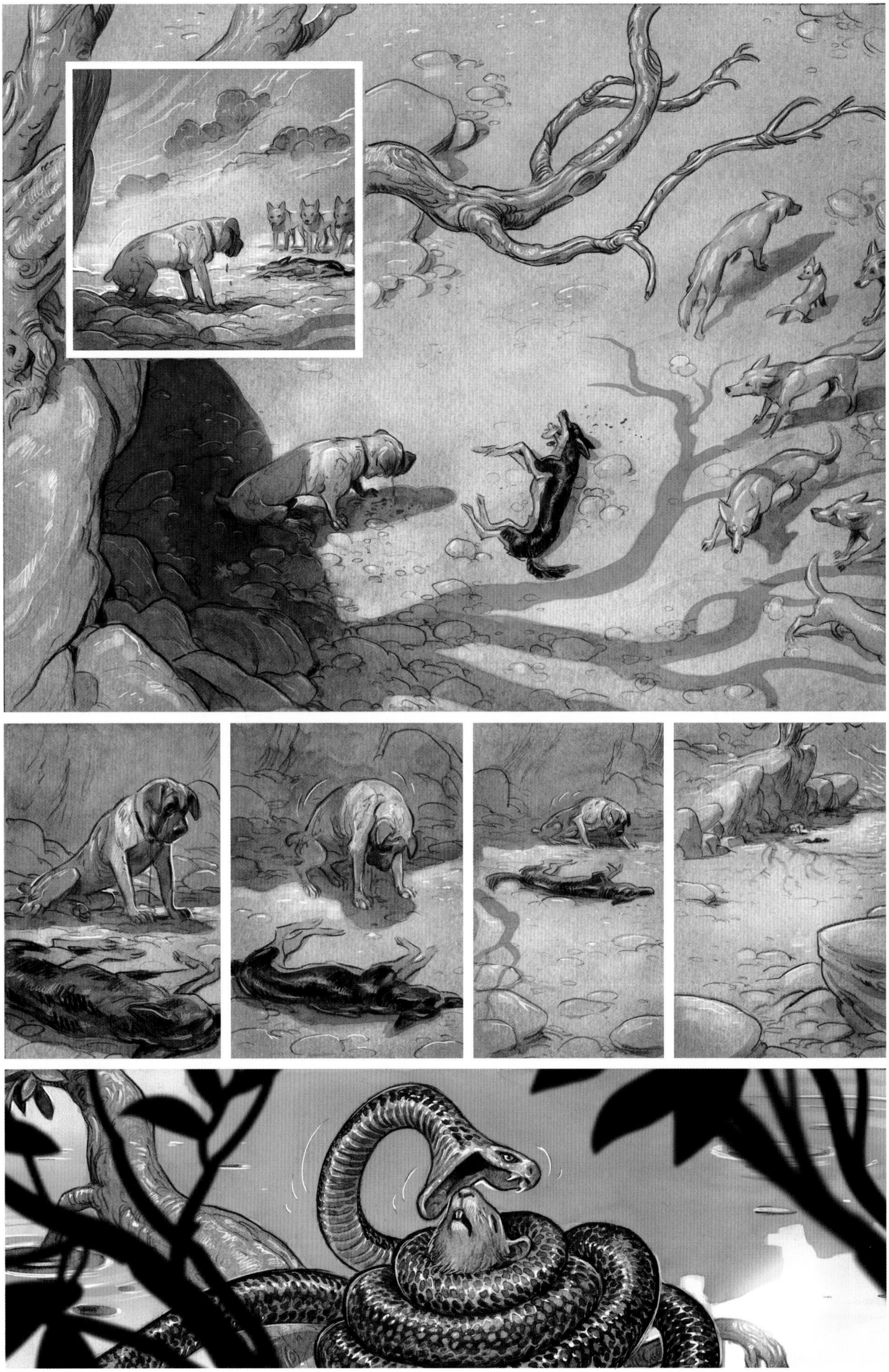

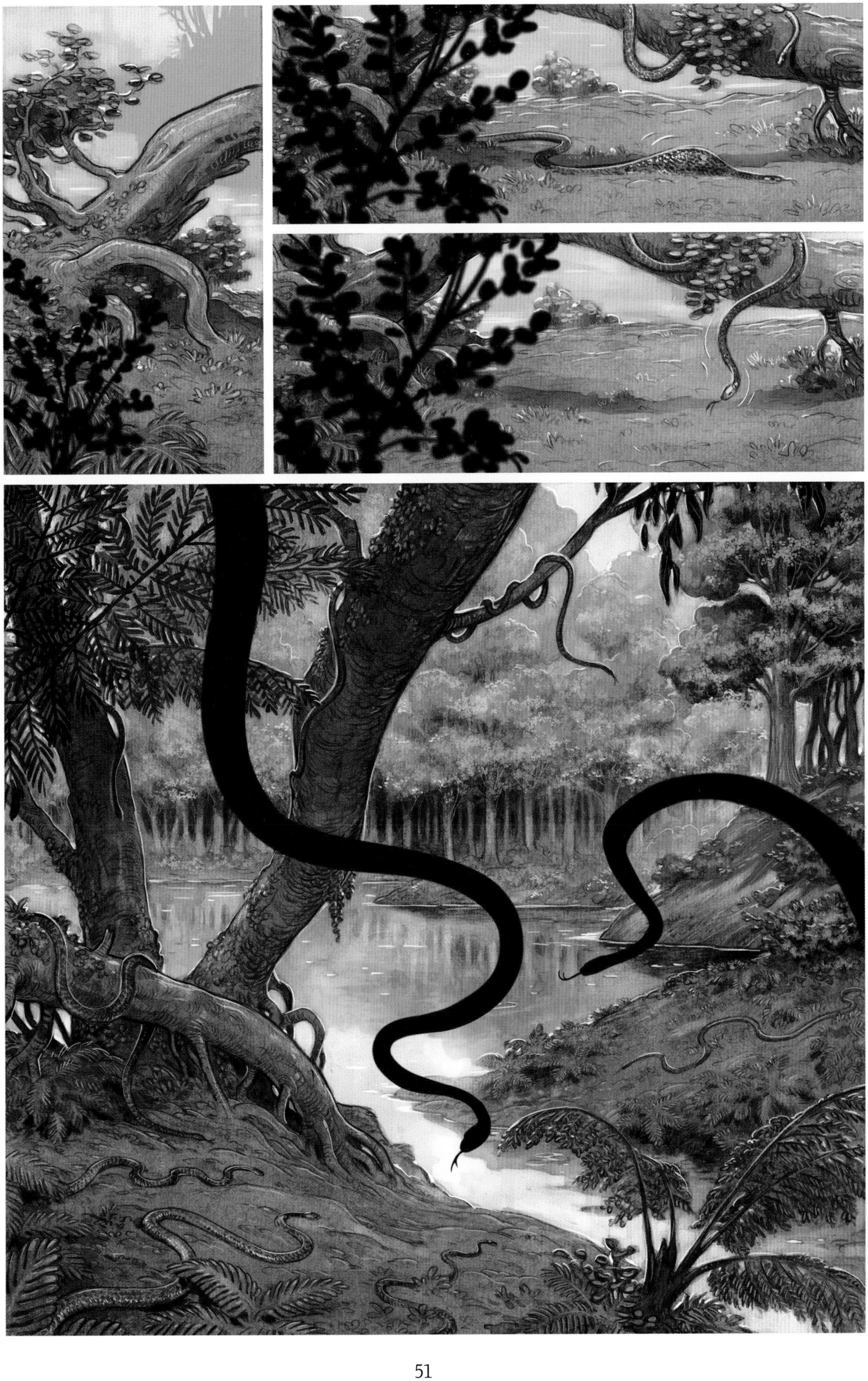

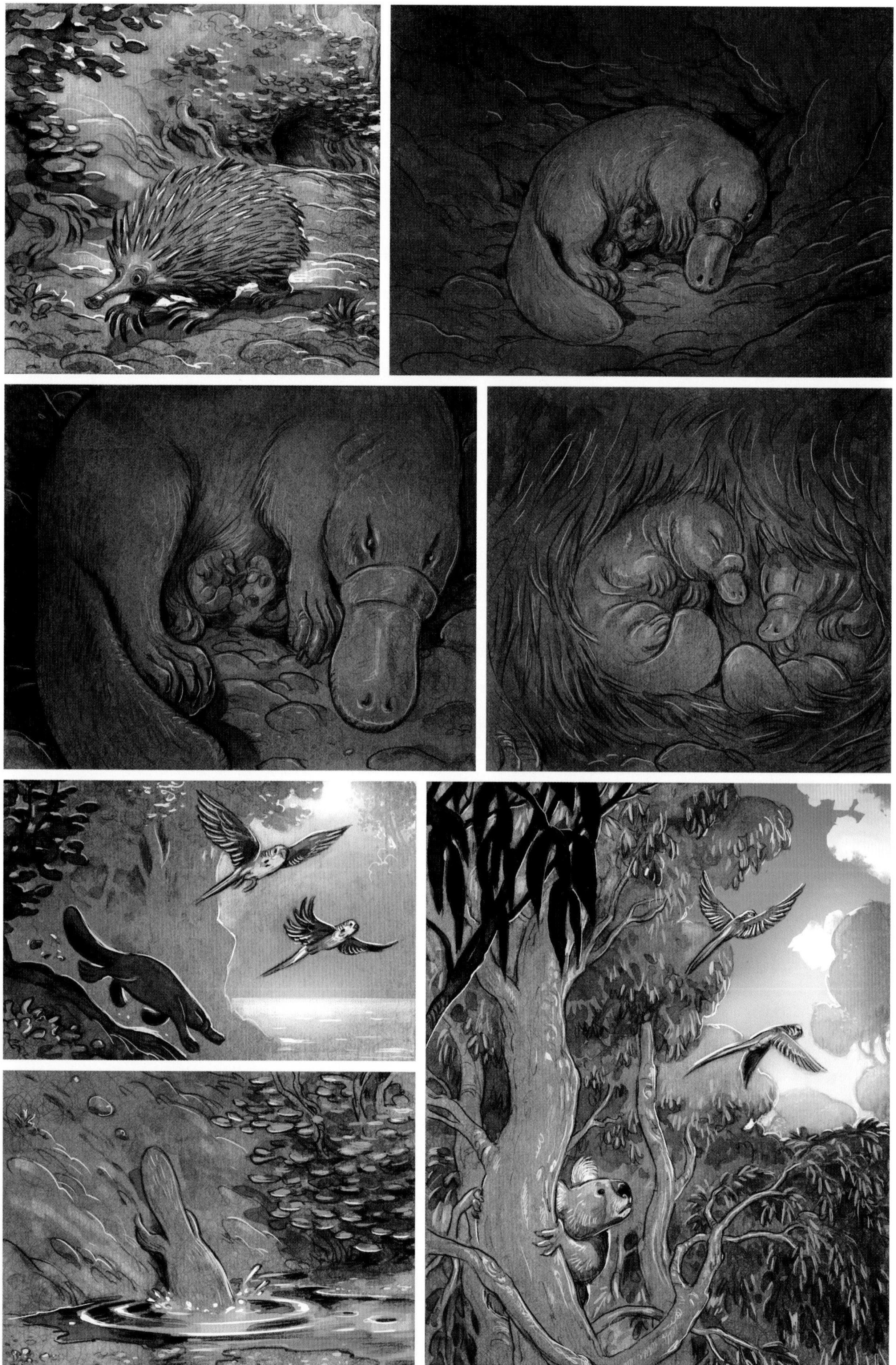

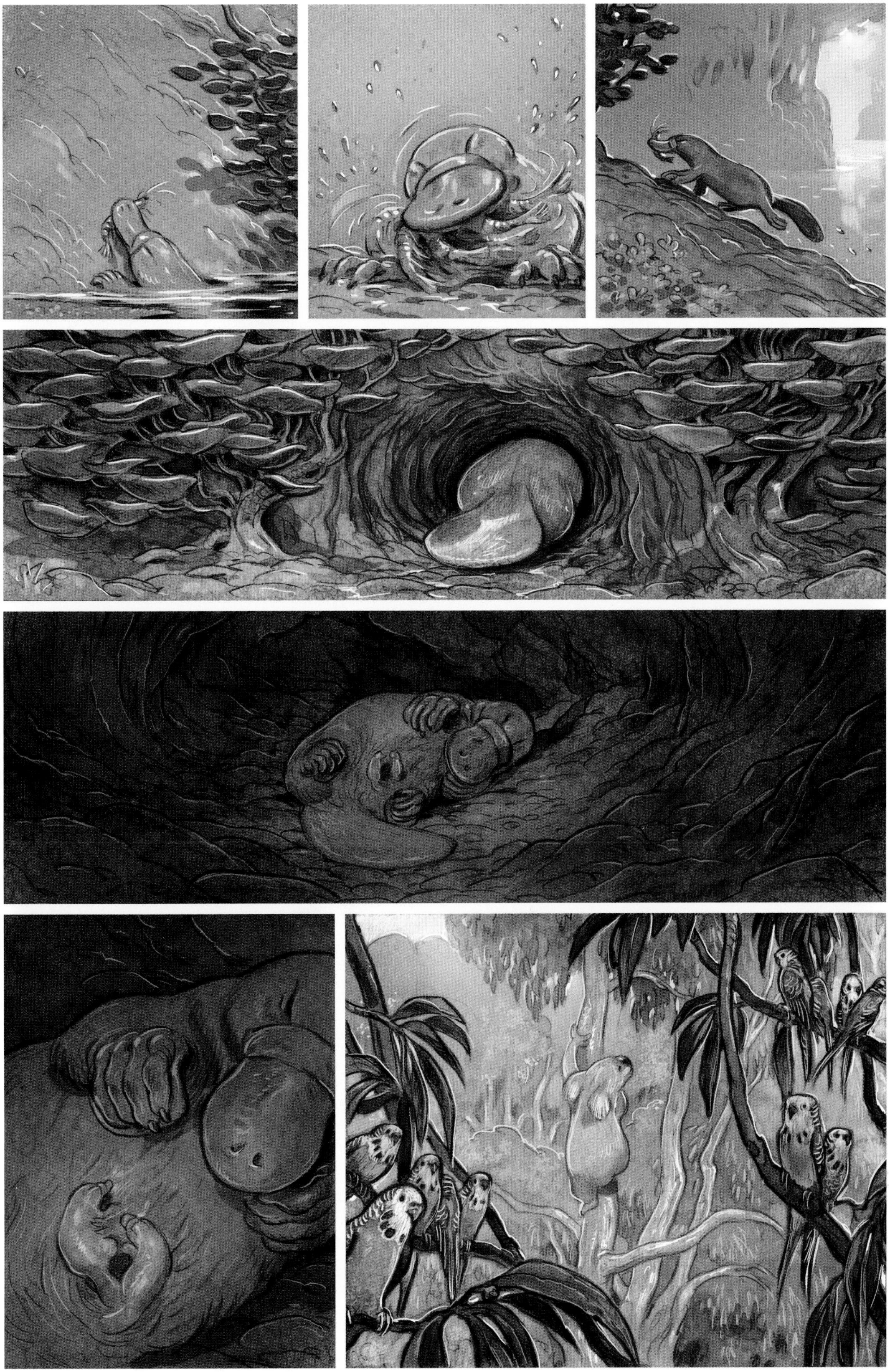

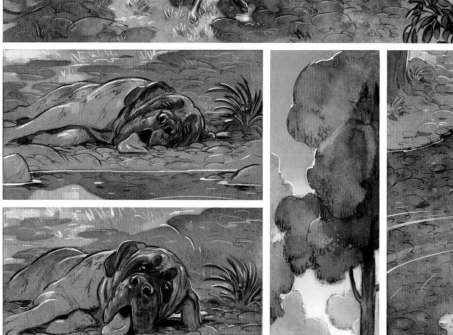

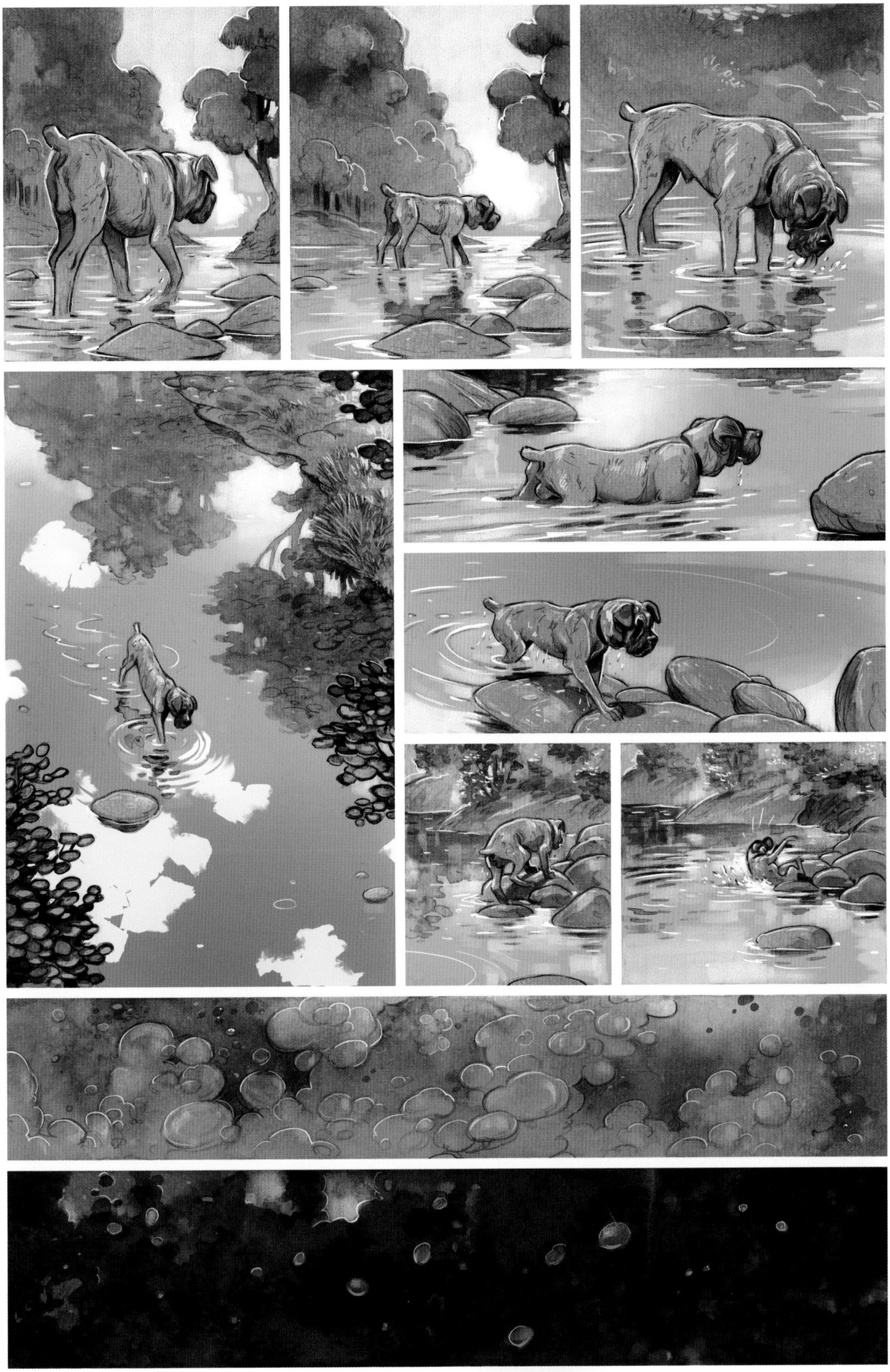

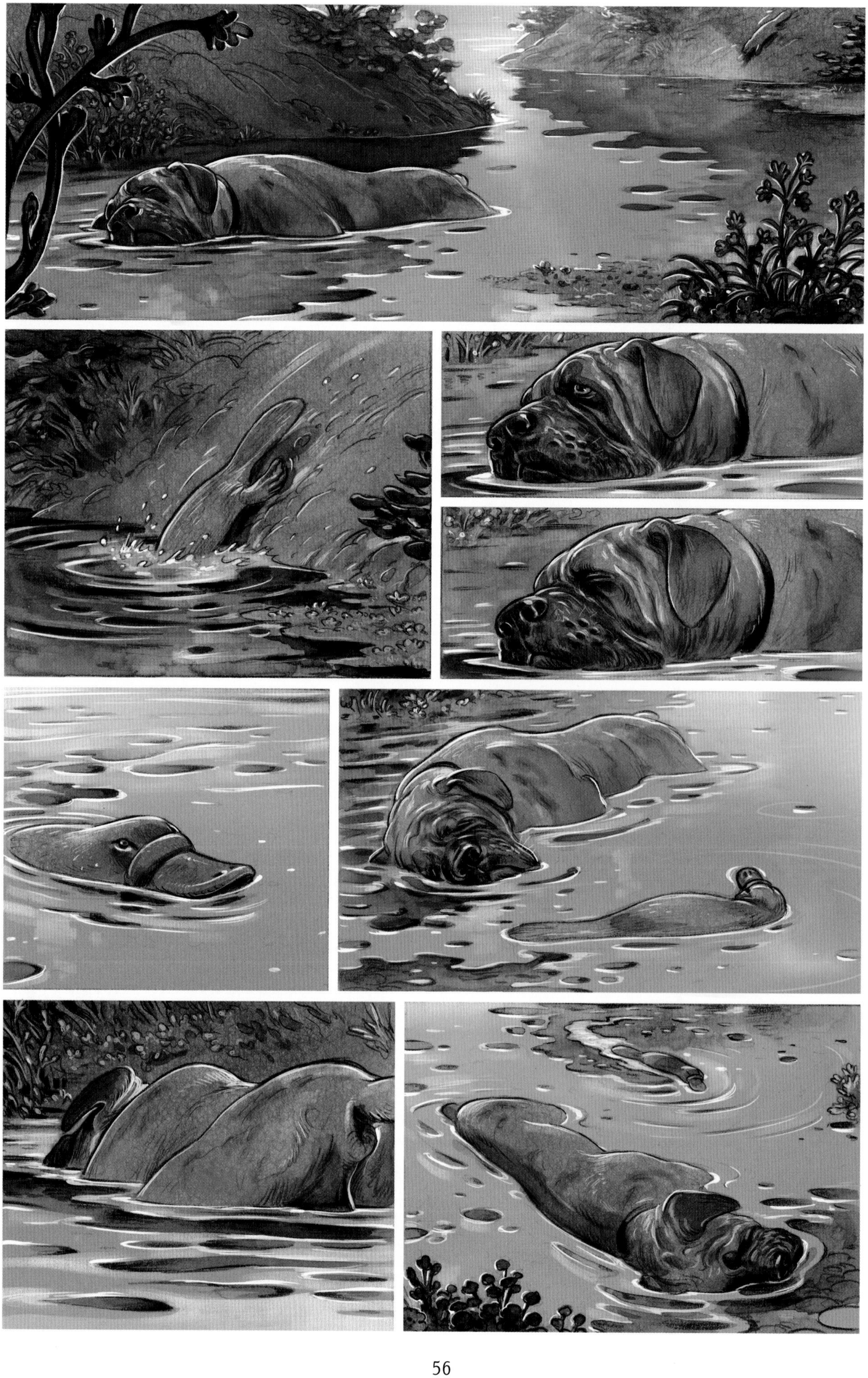

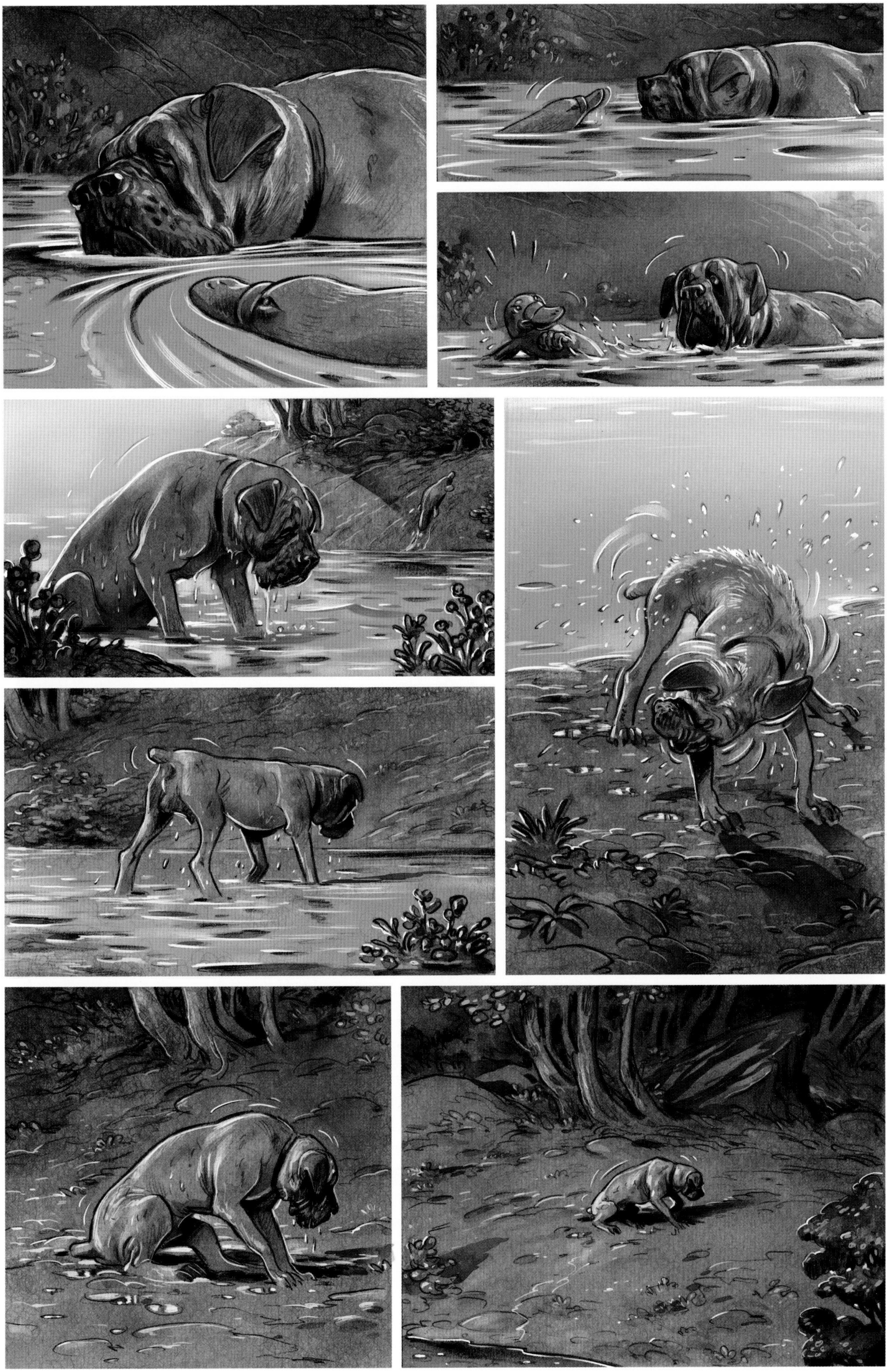

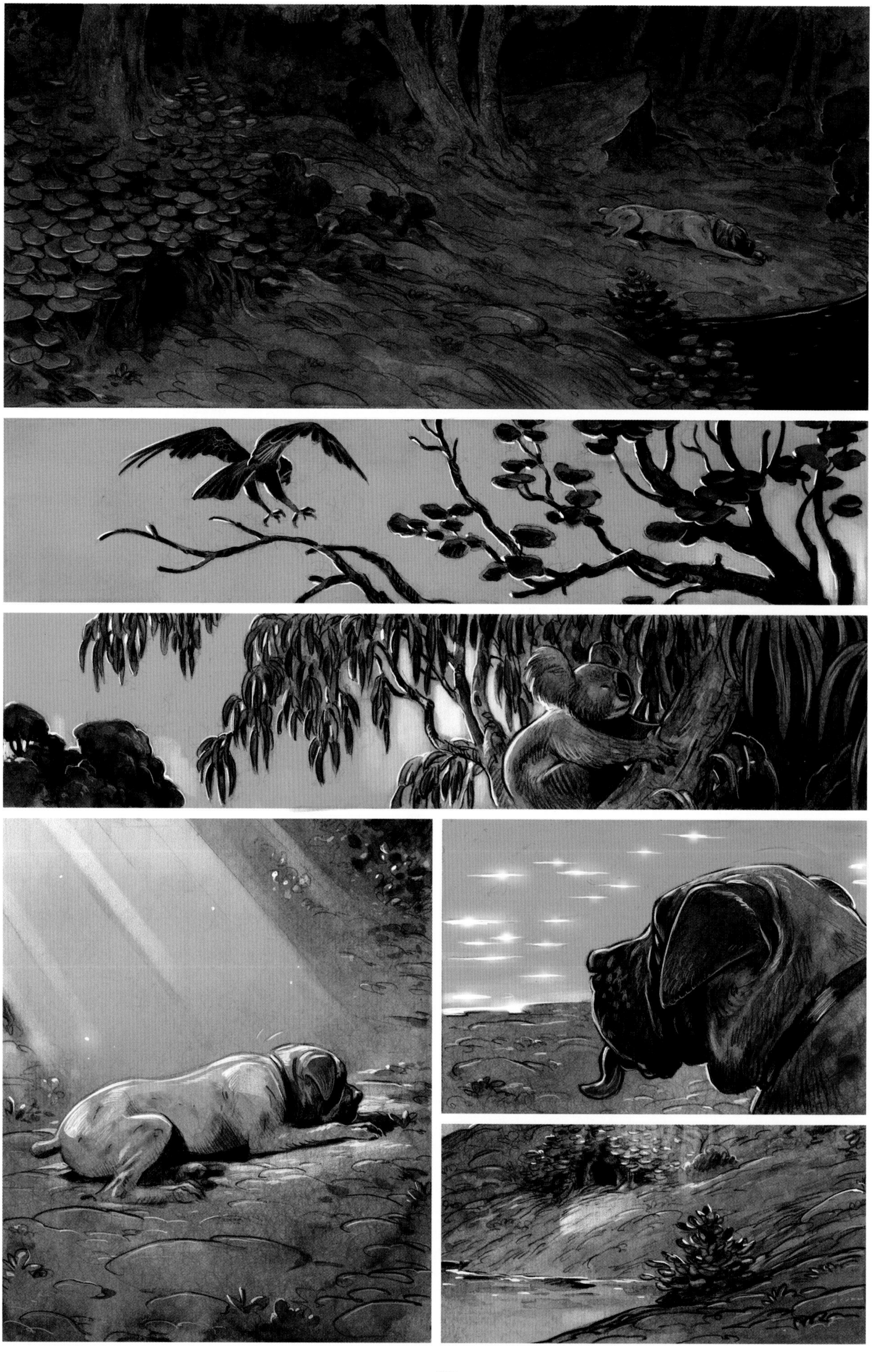

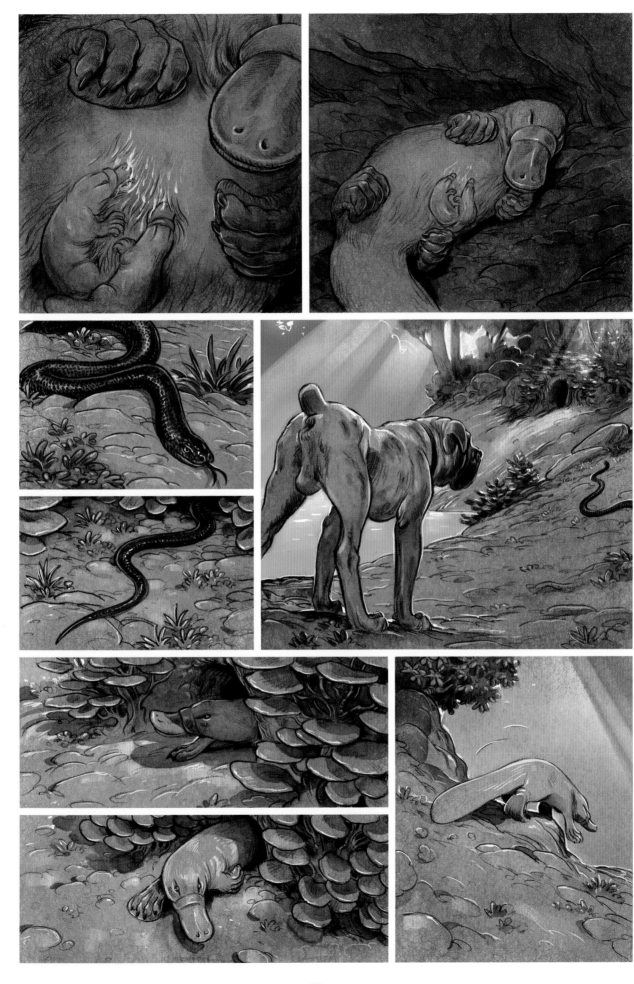

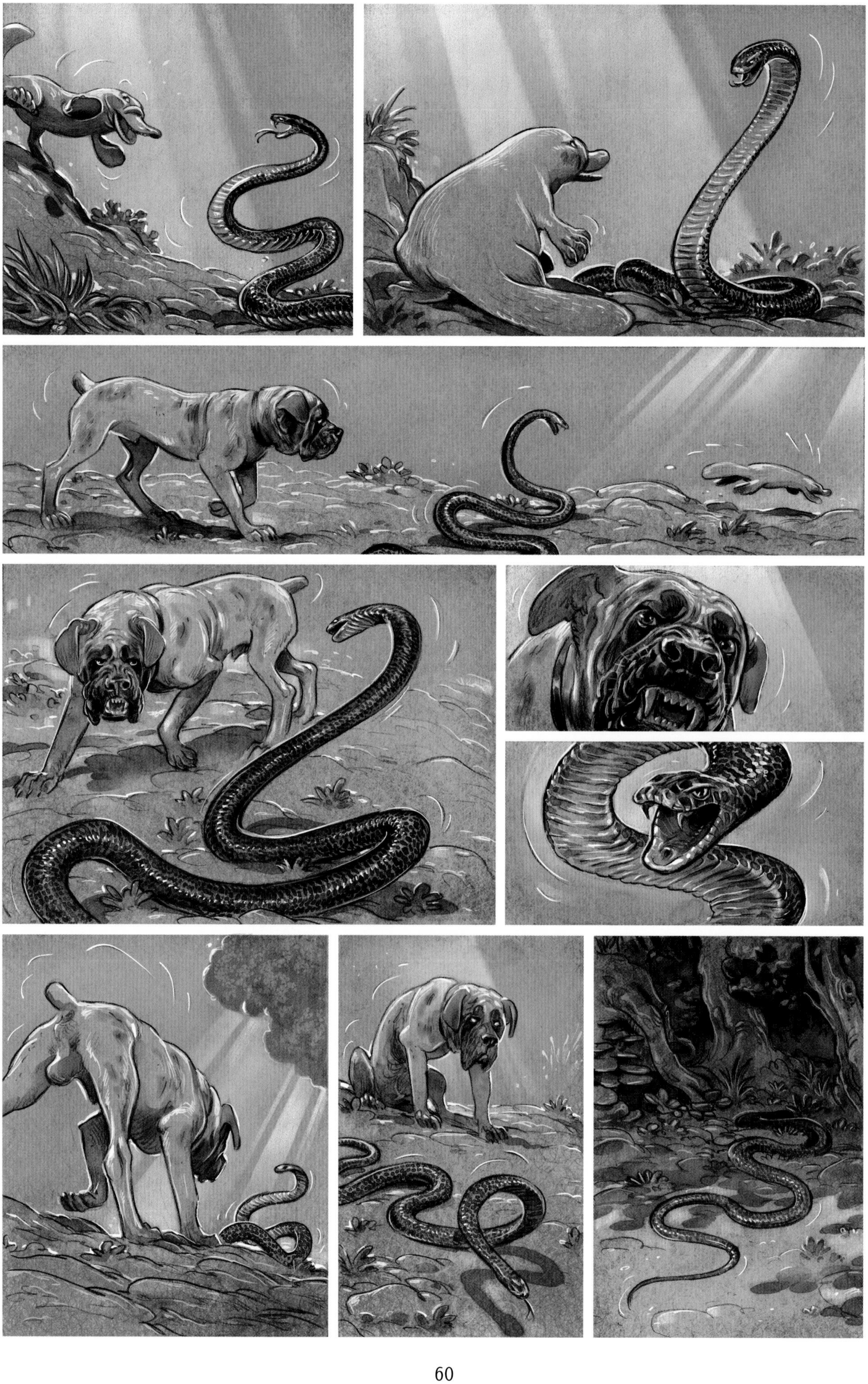

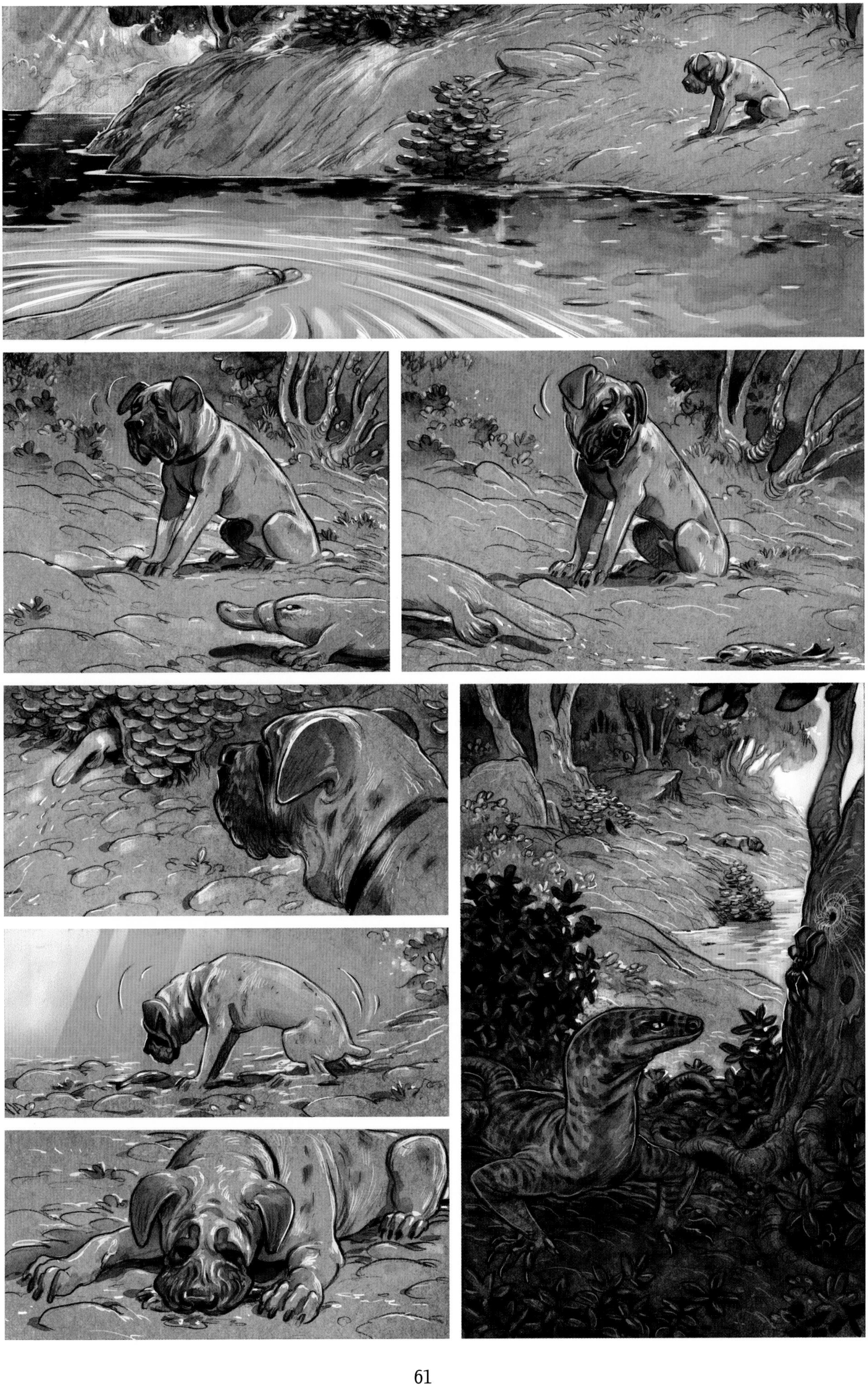

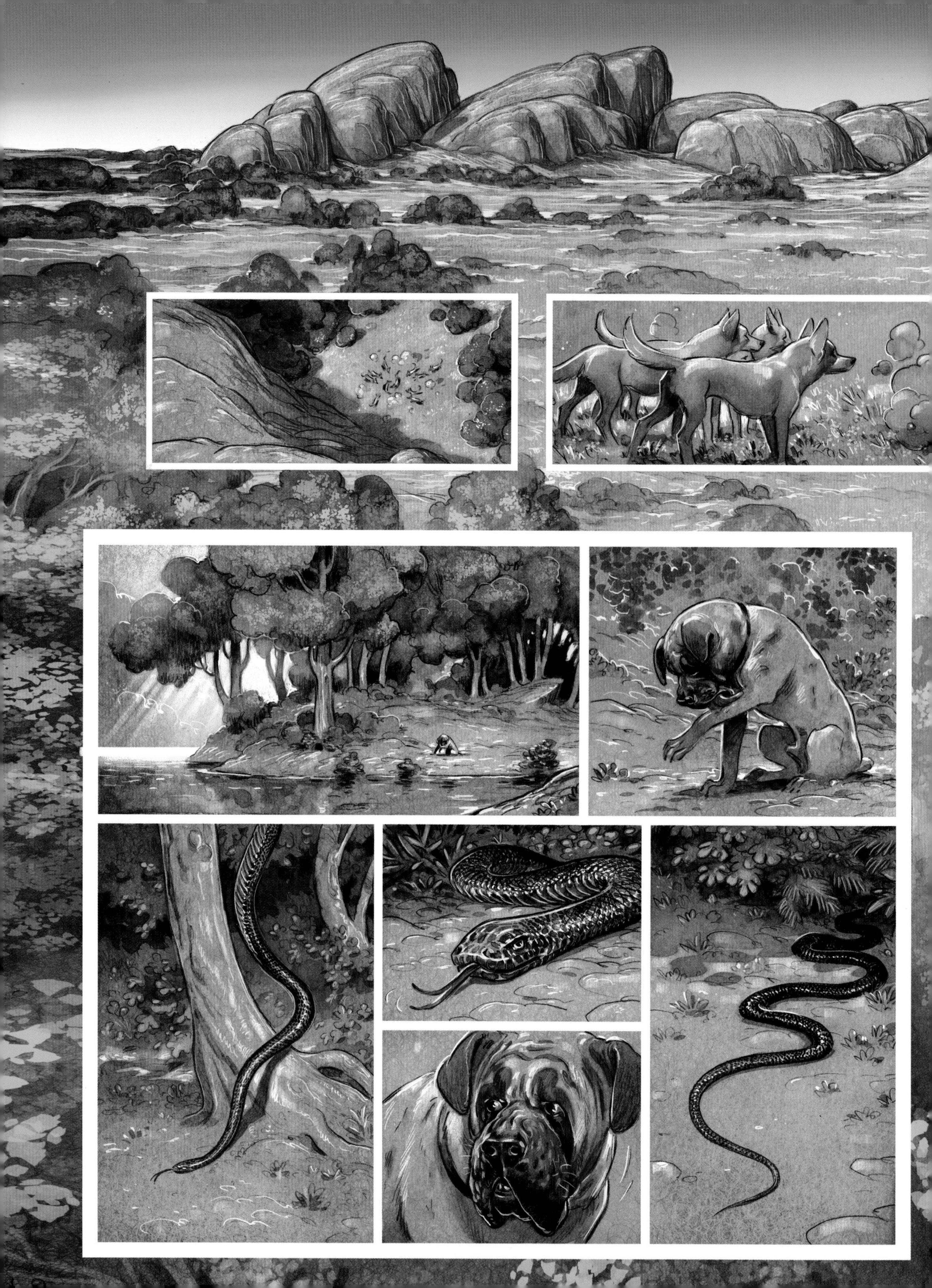

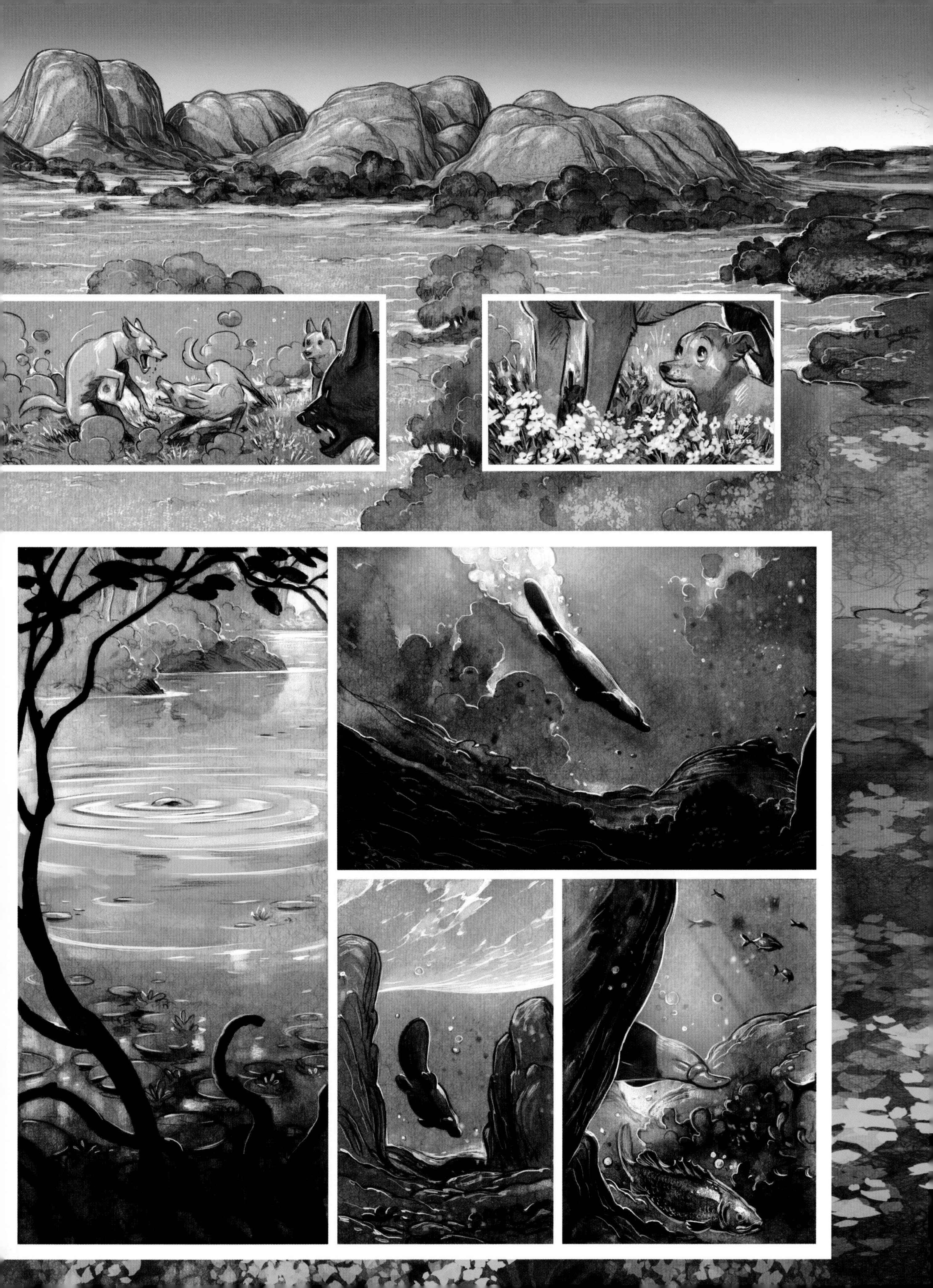

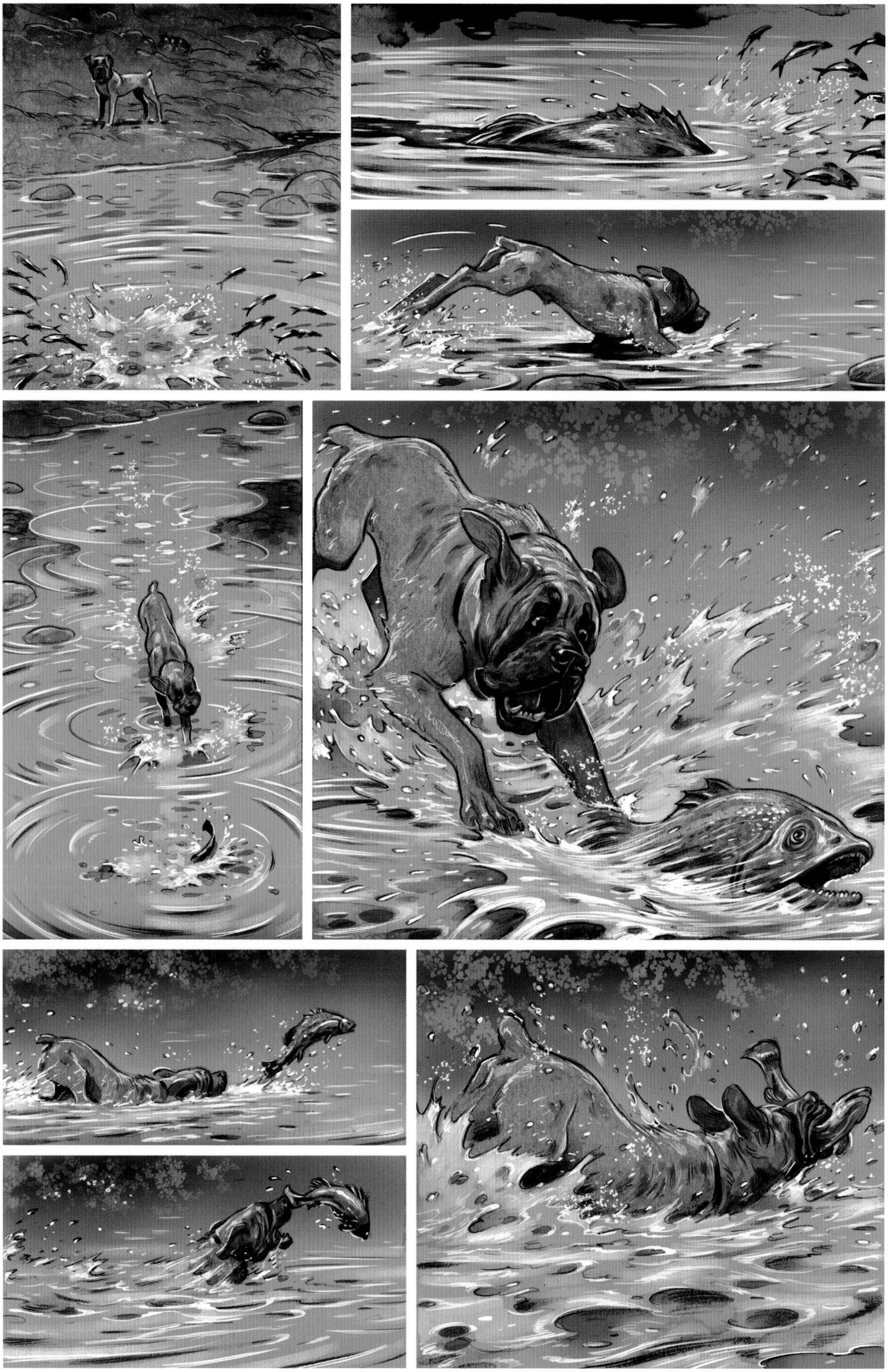

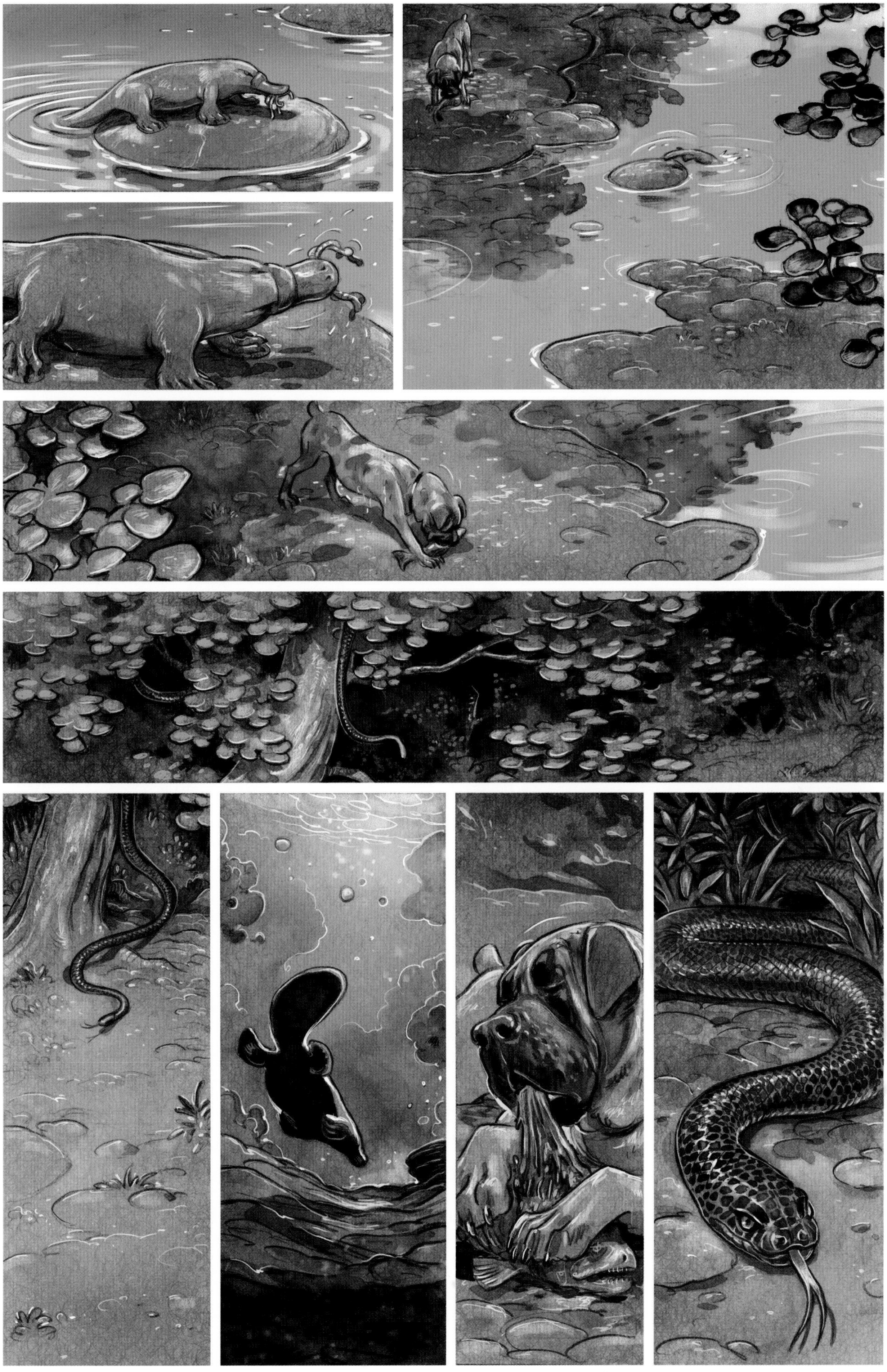

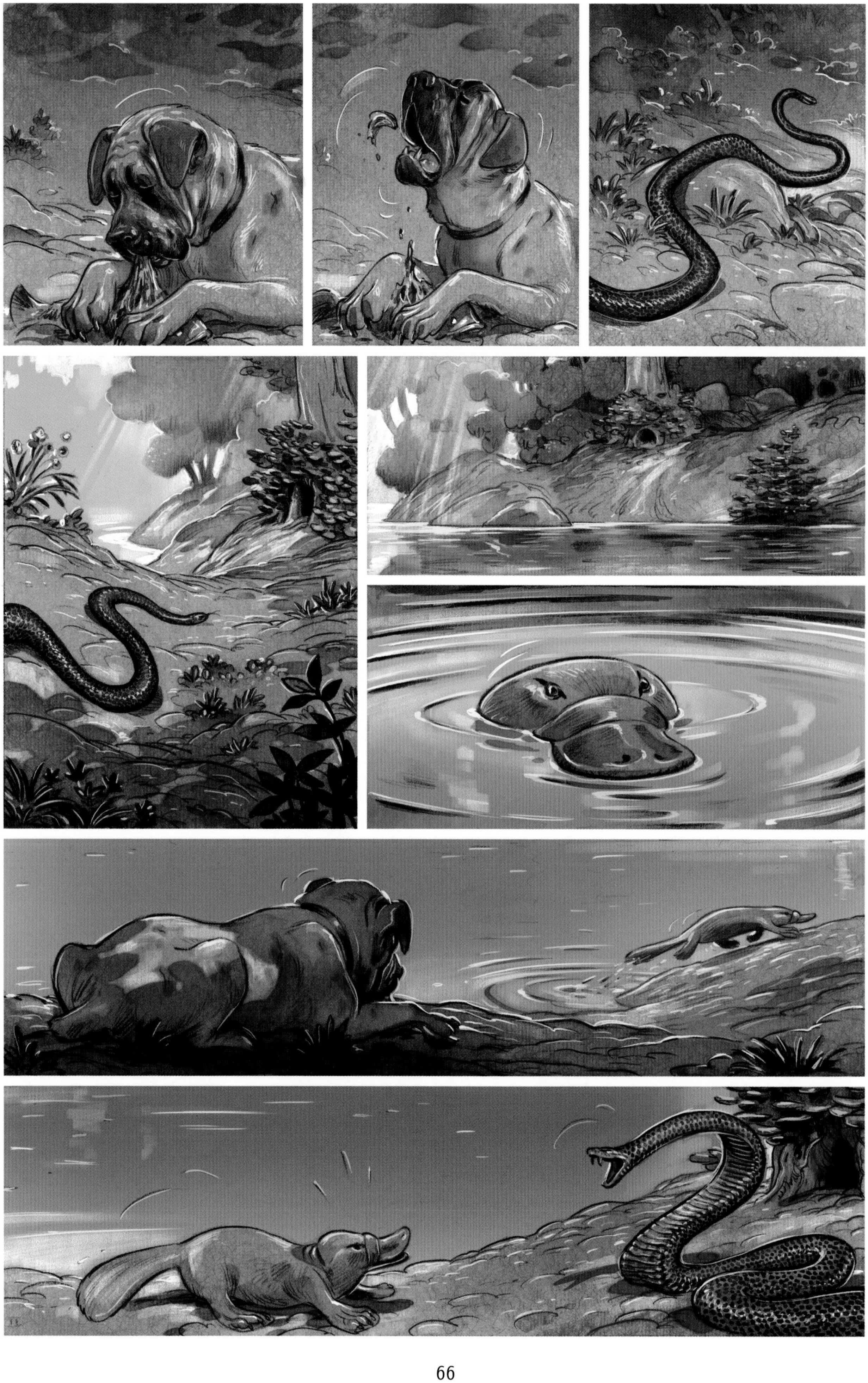

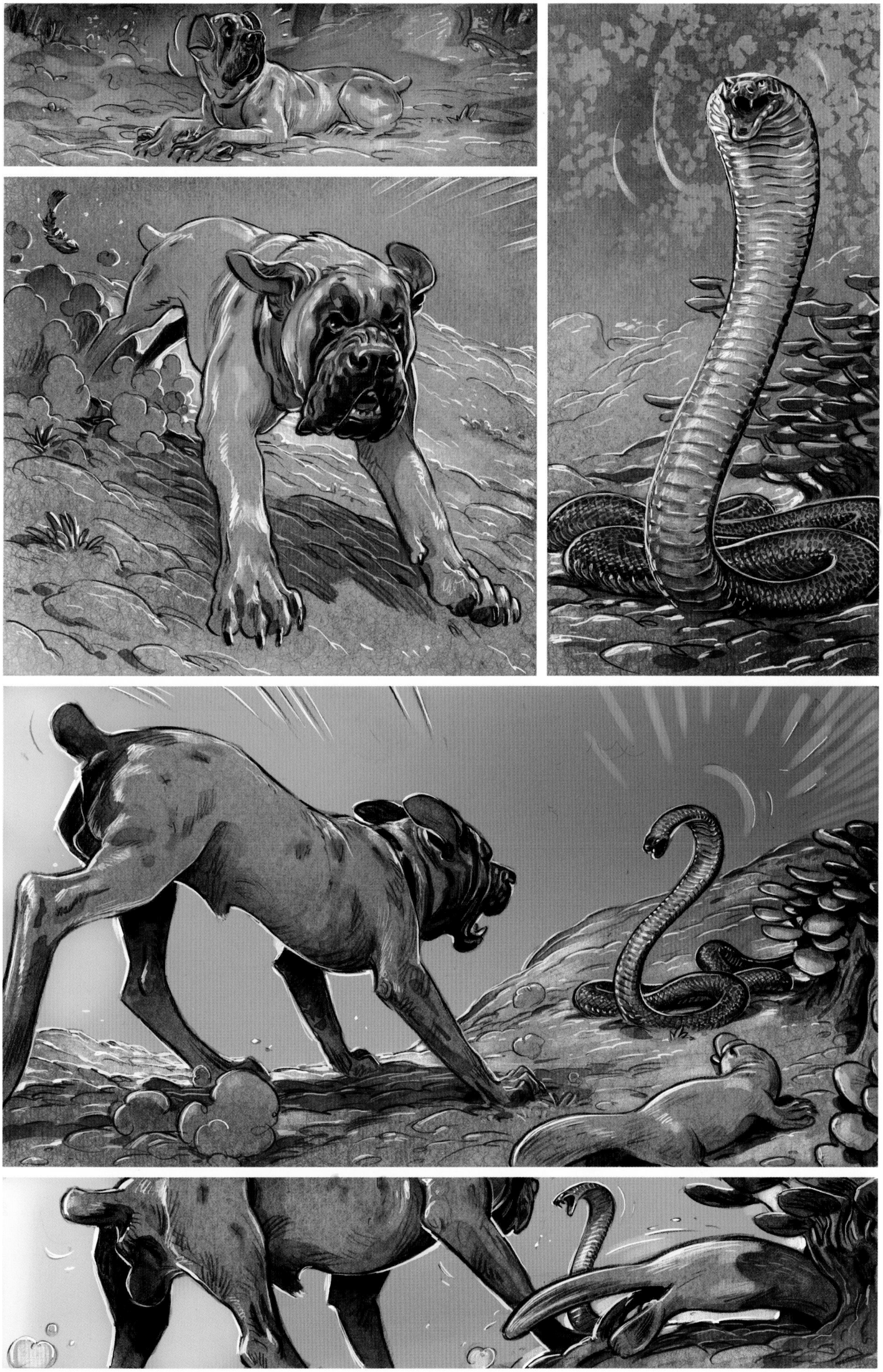

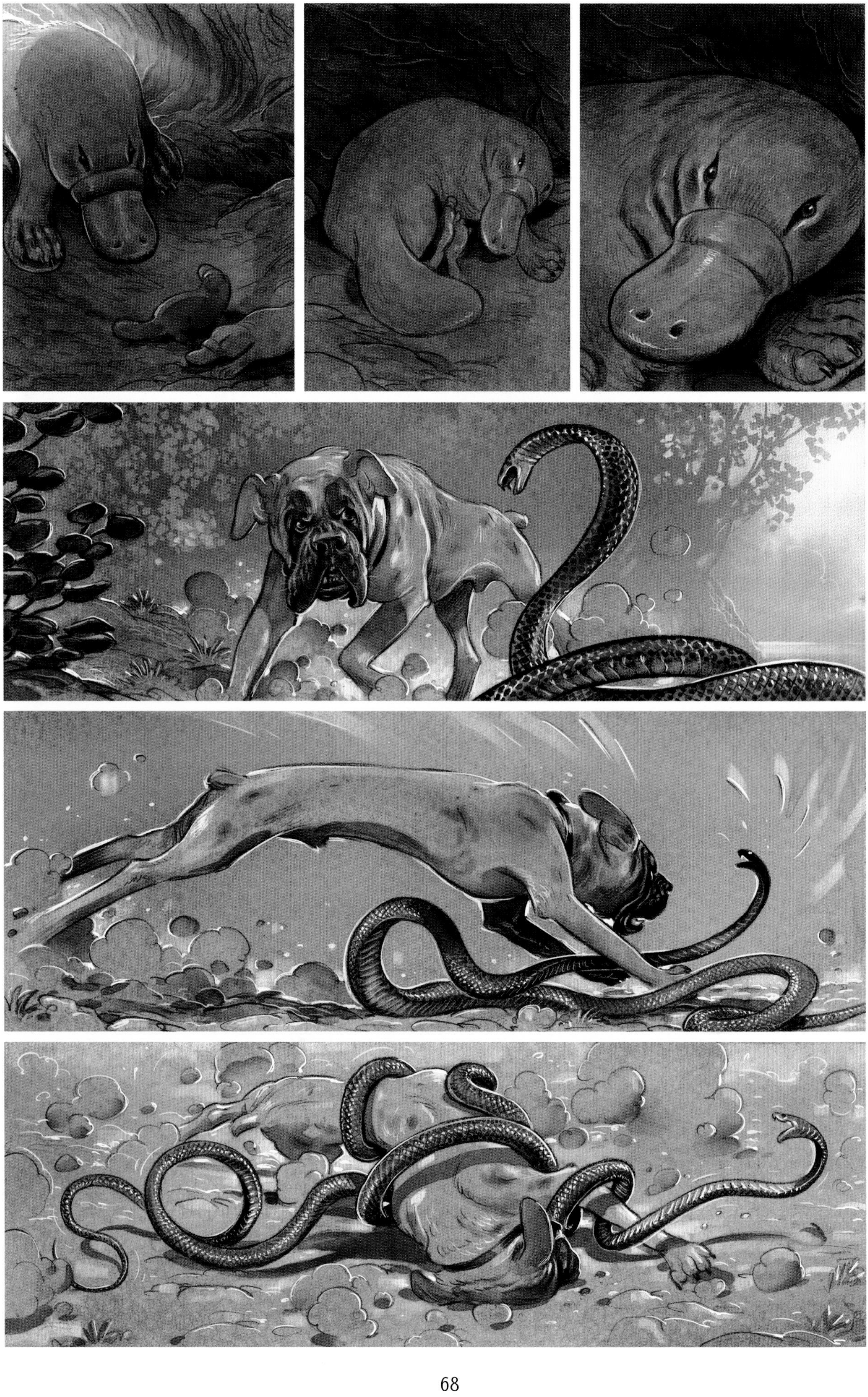

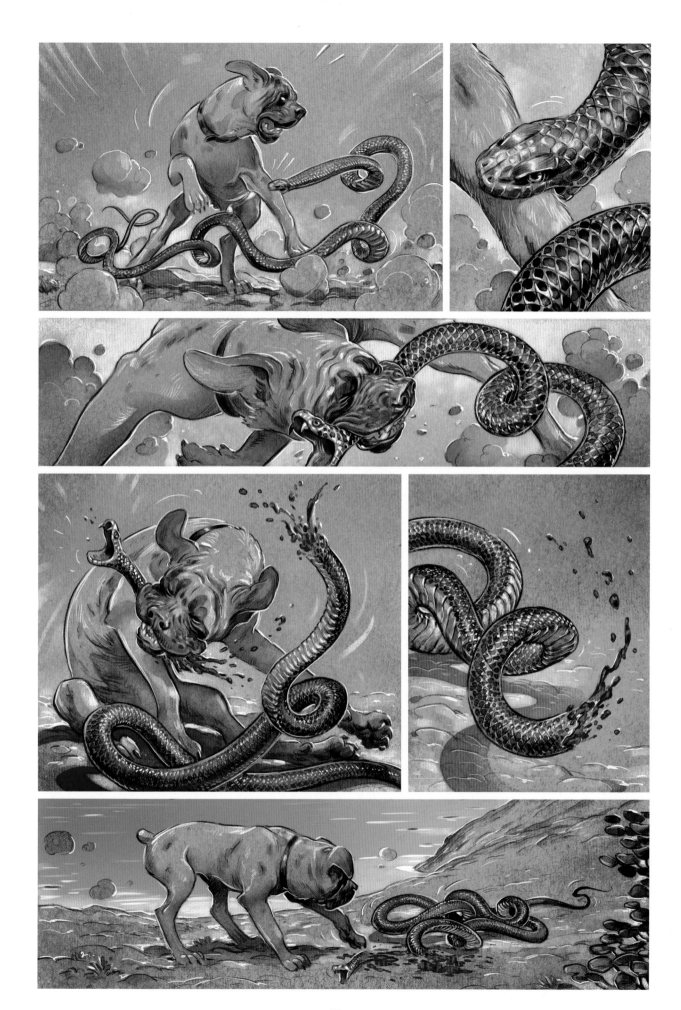

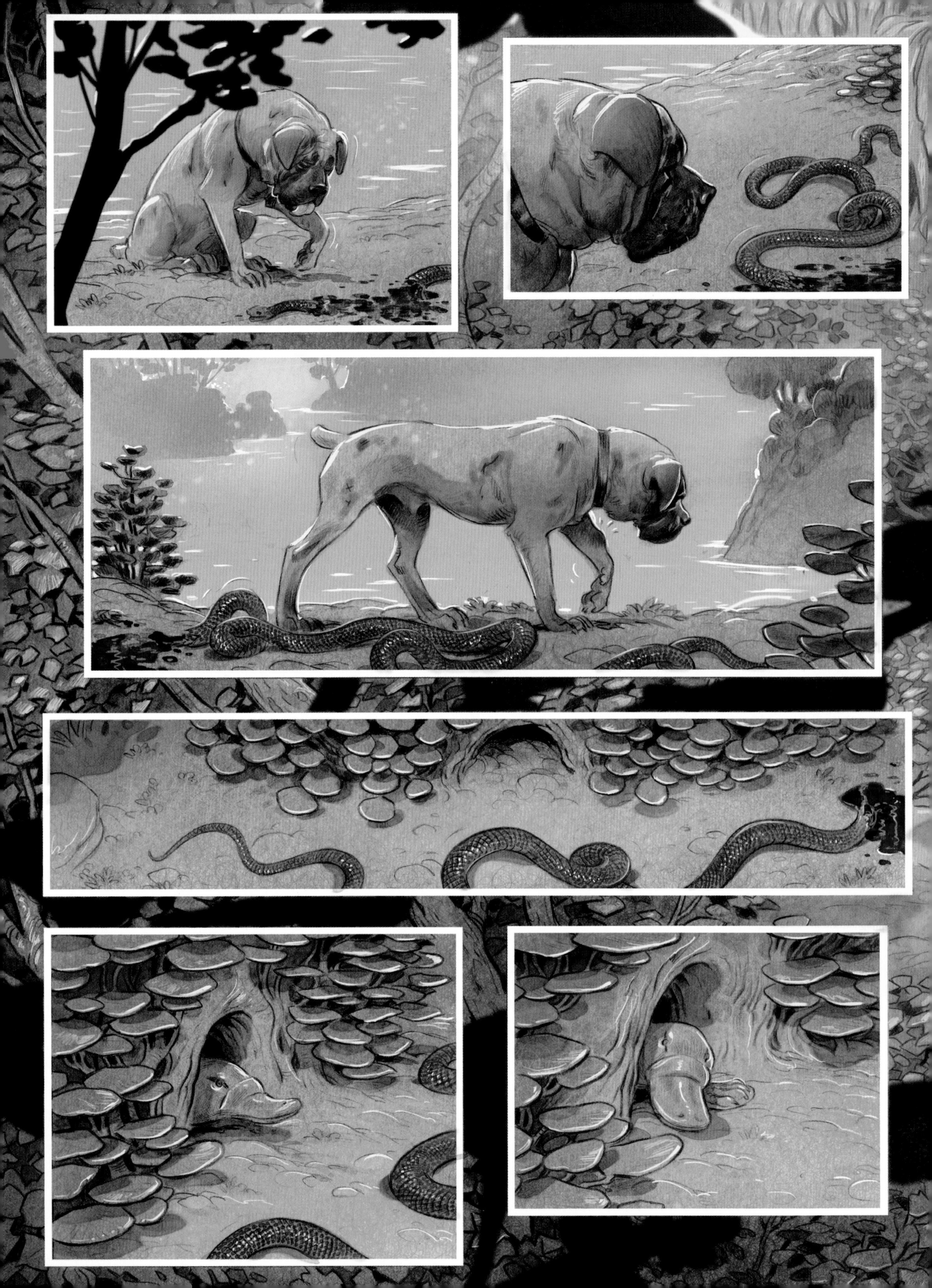

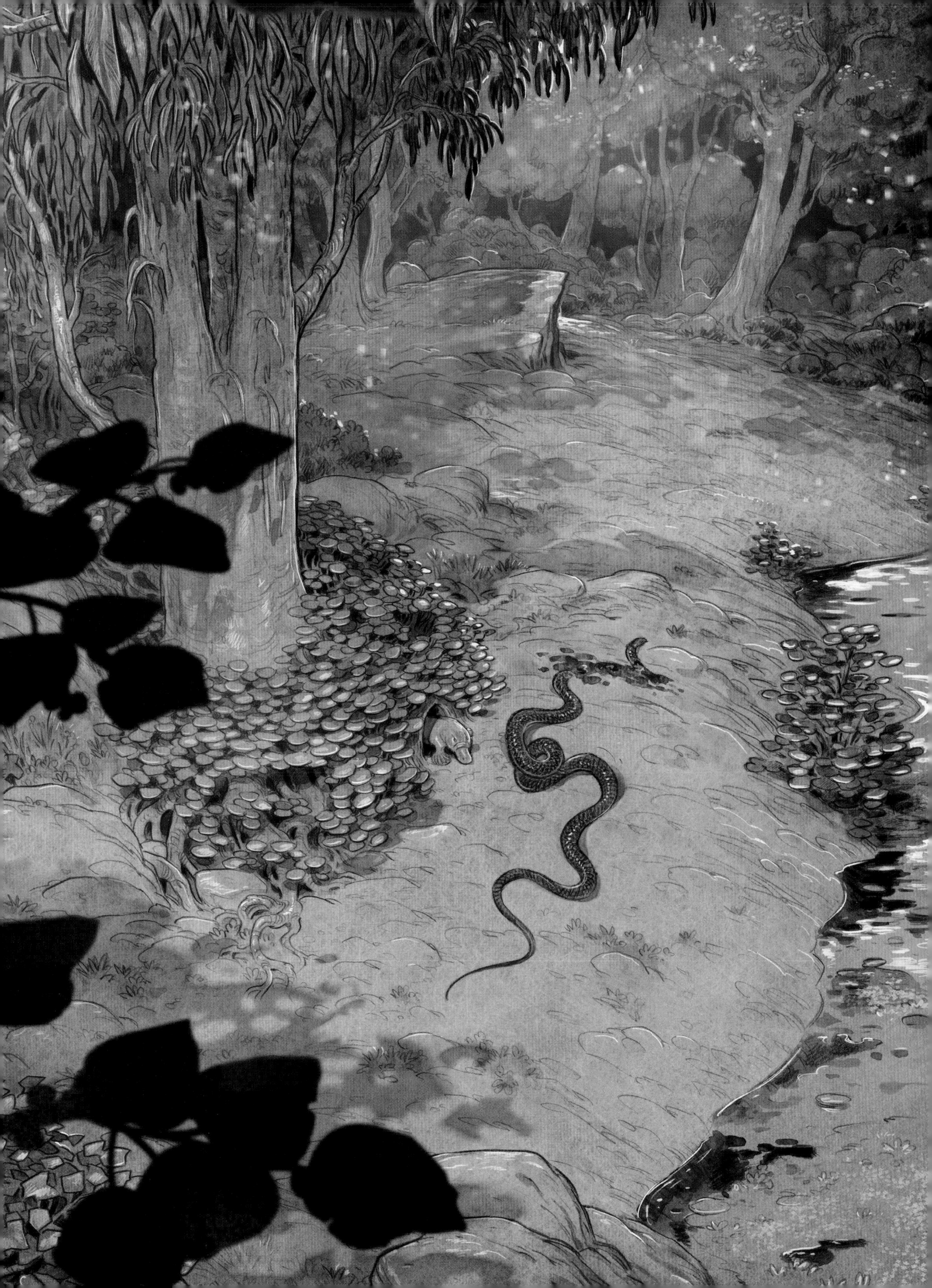

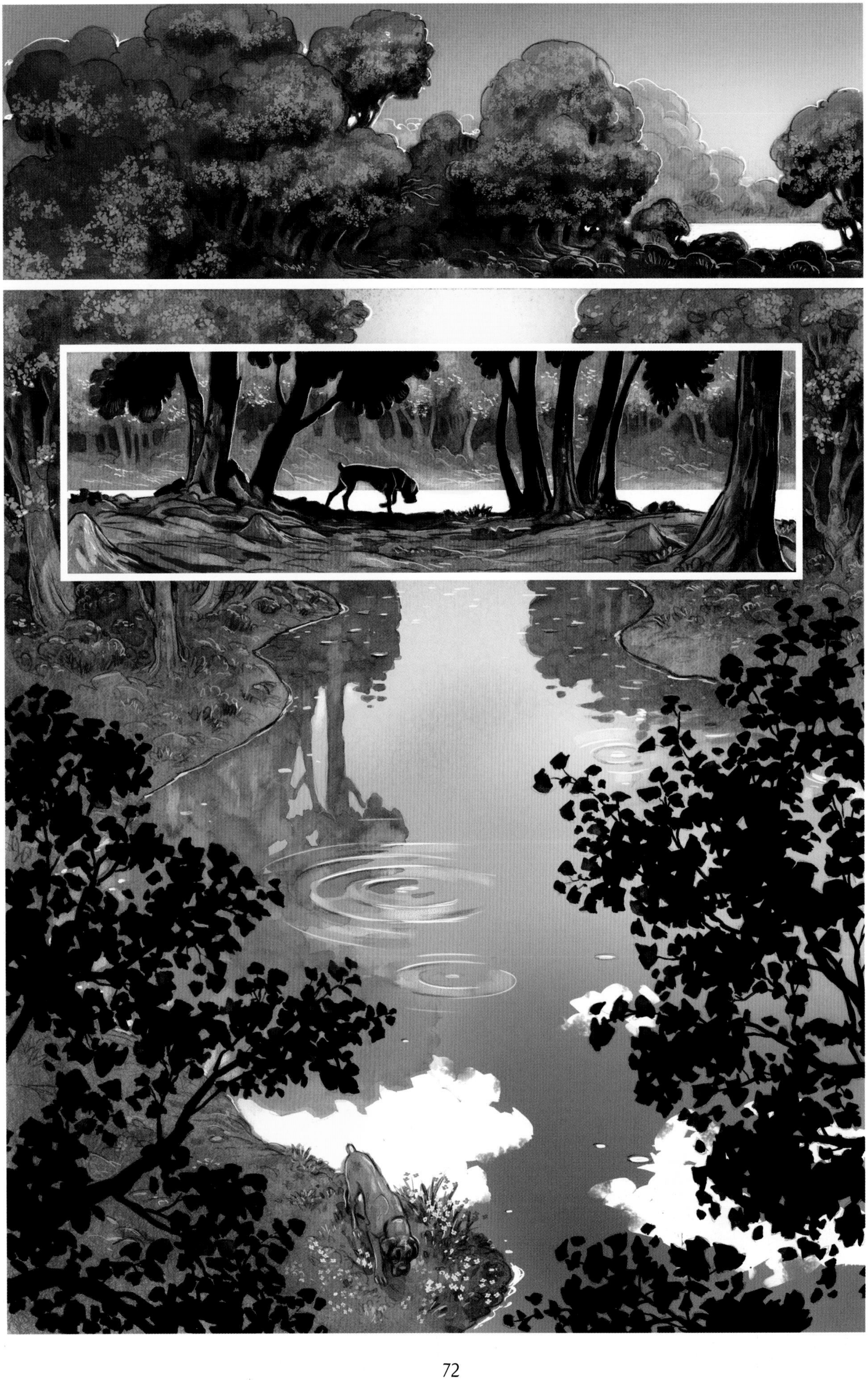

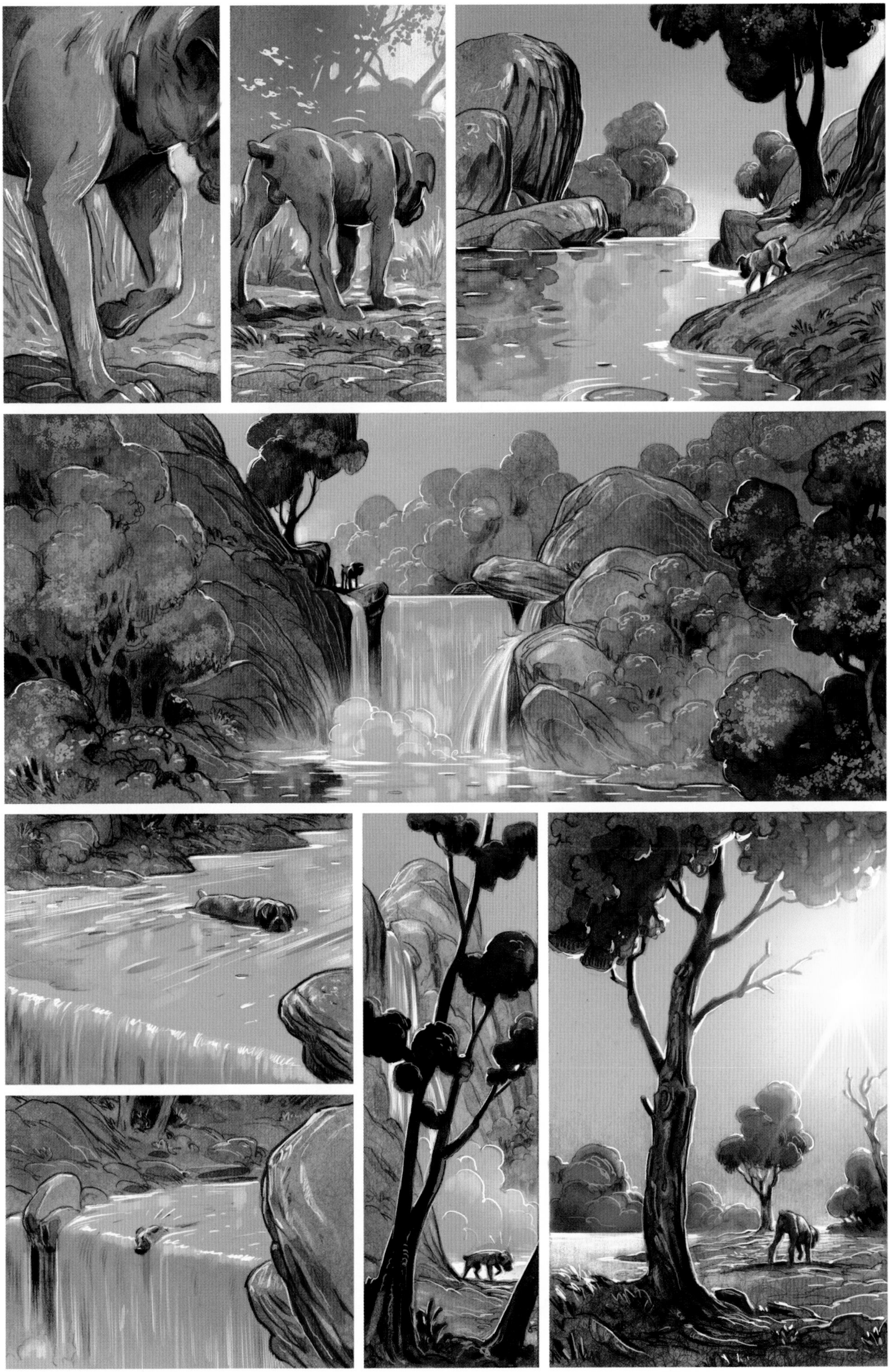

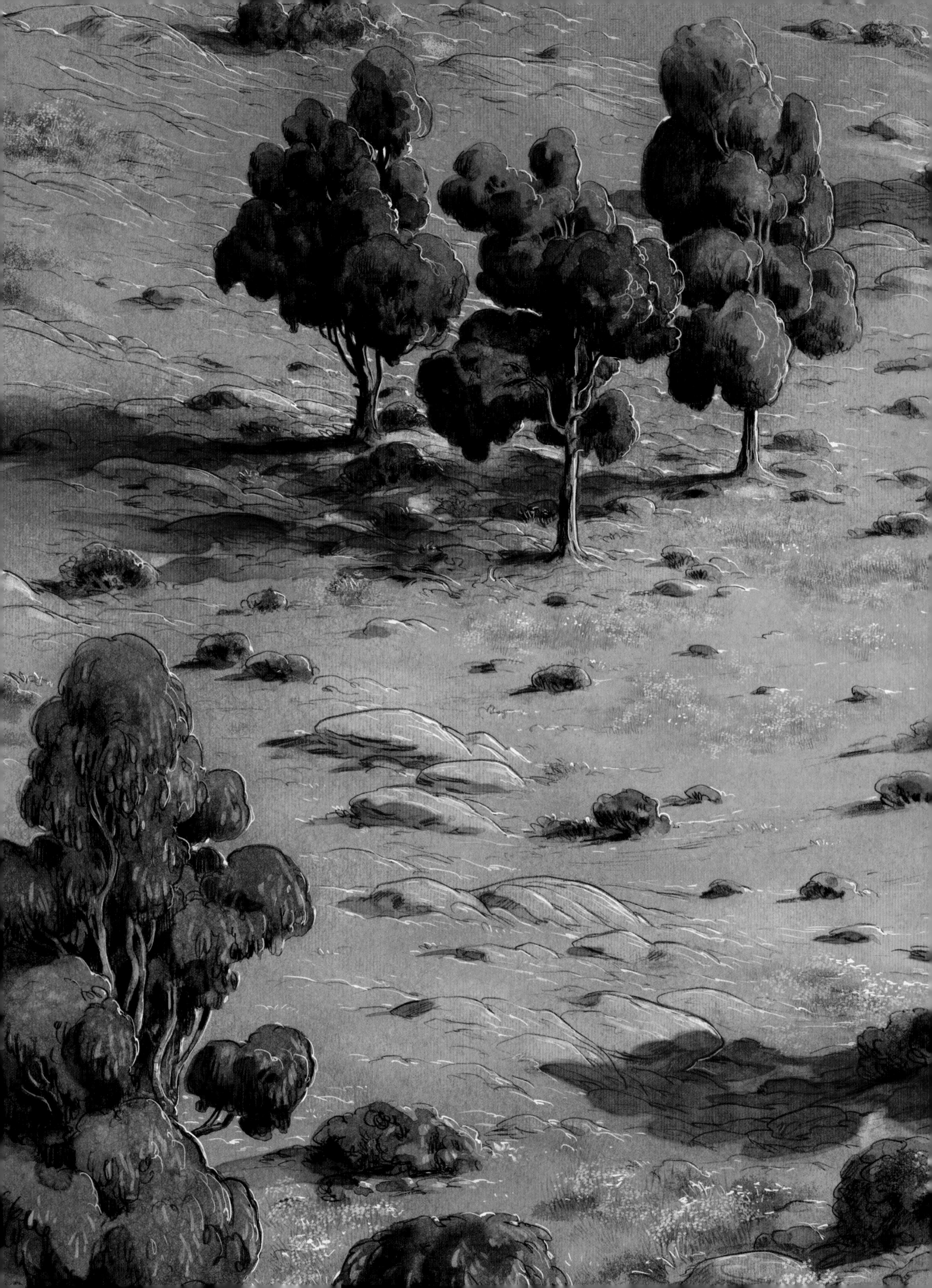

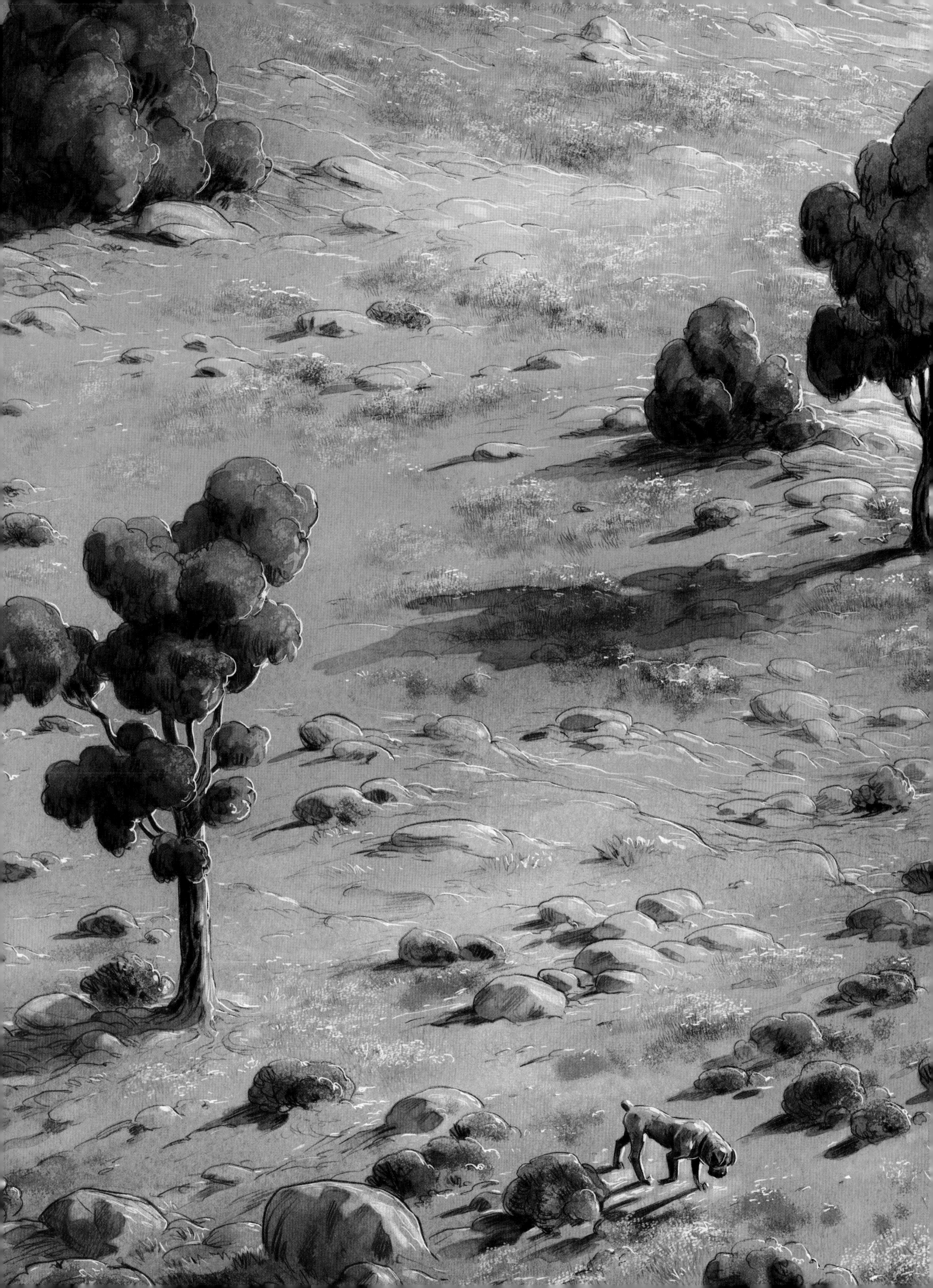

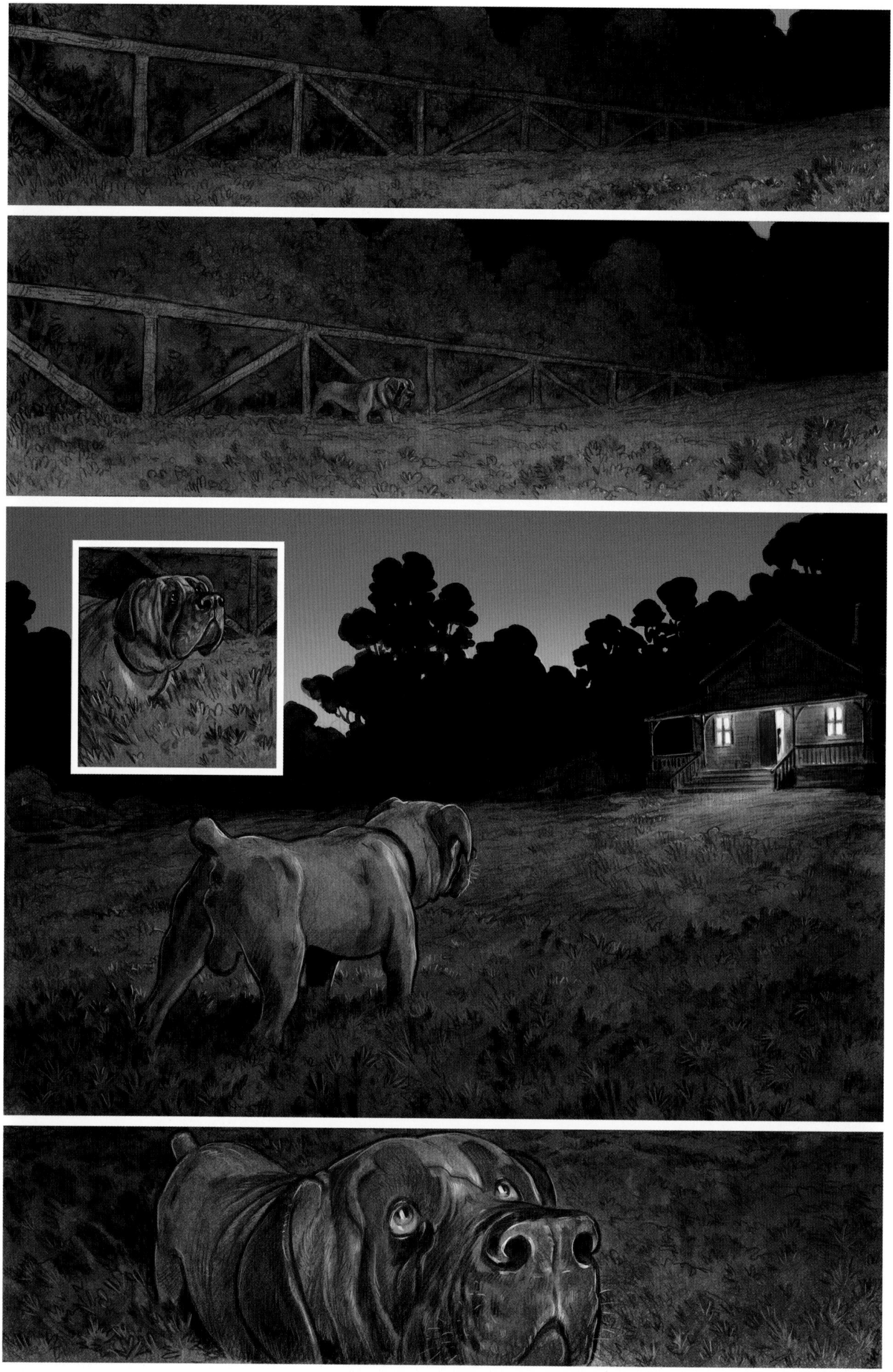

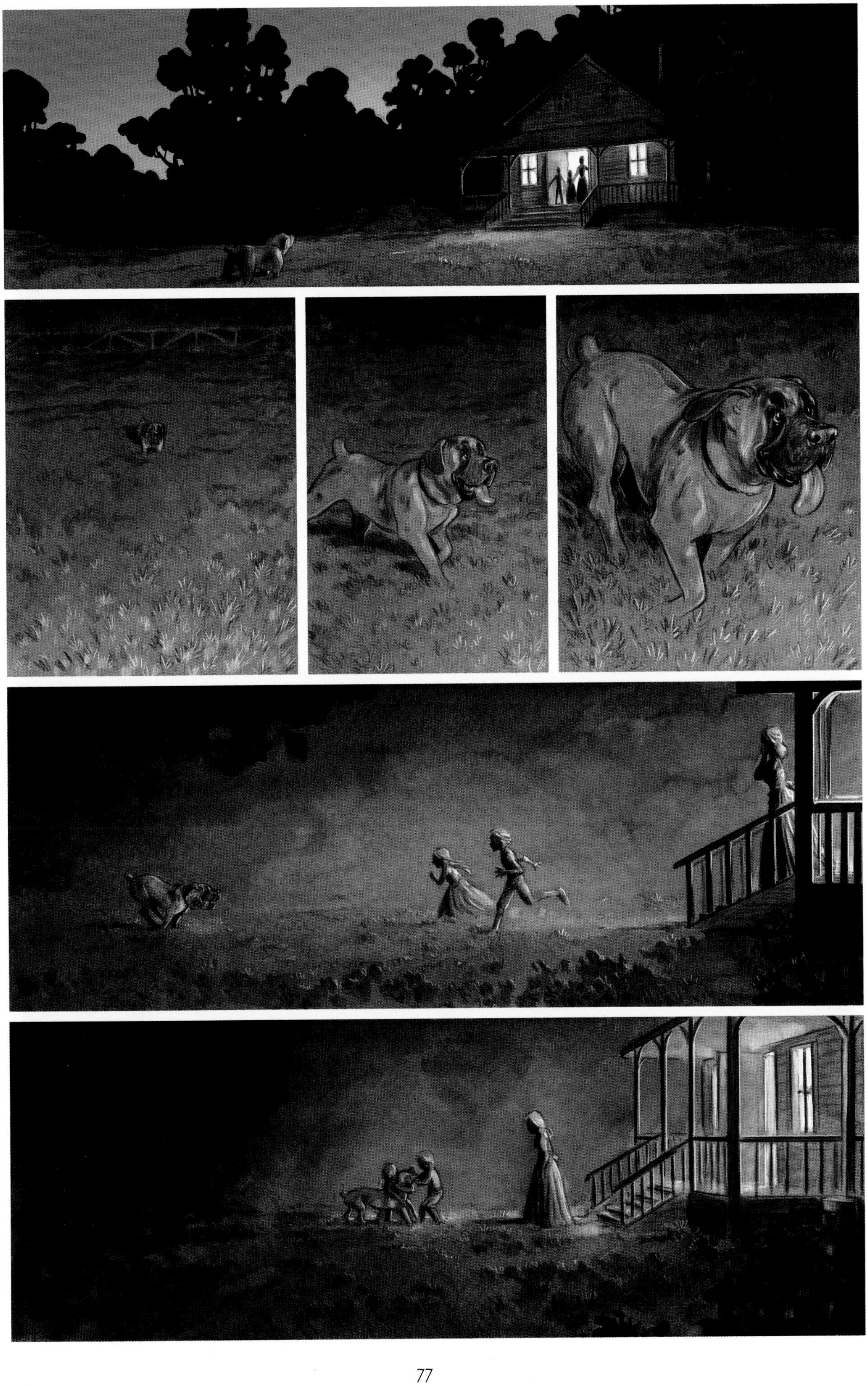

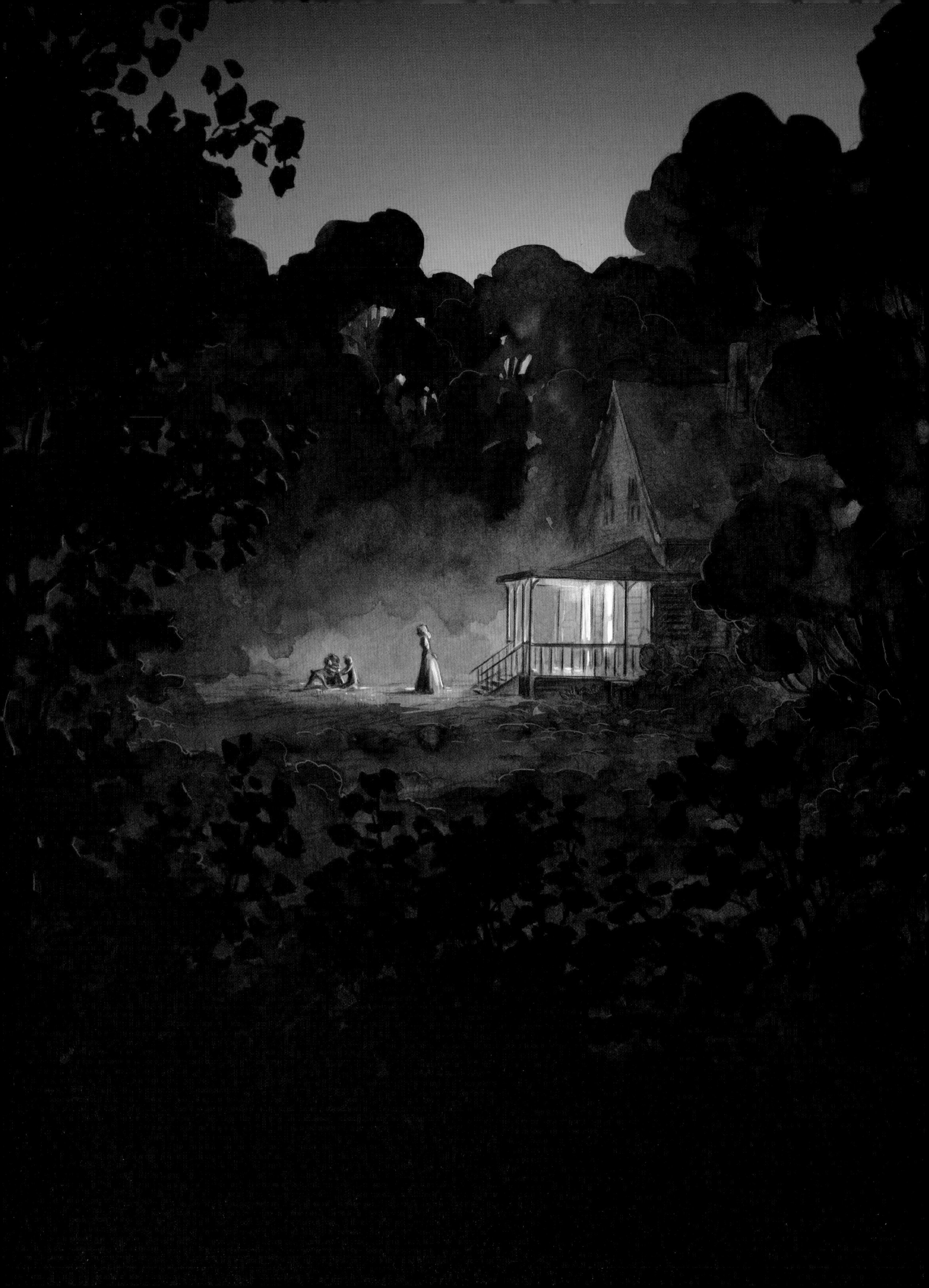

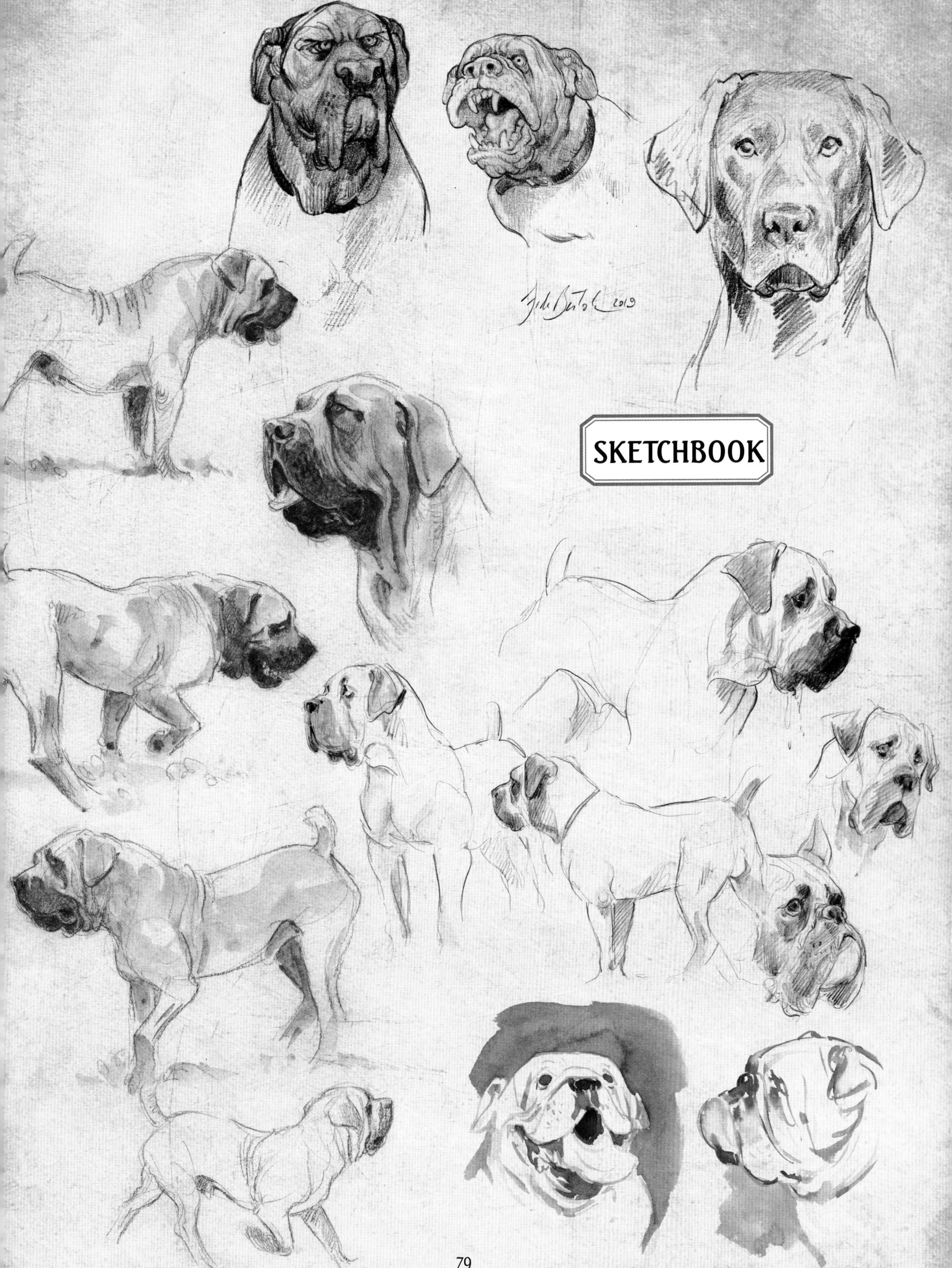
SKETCHBOOK
2019

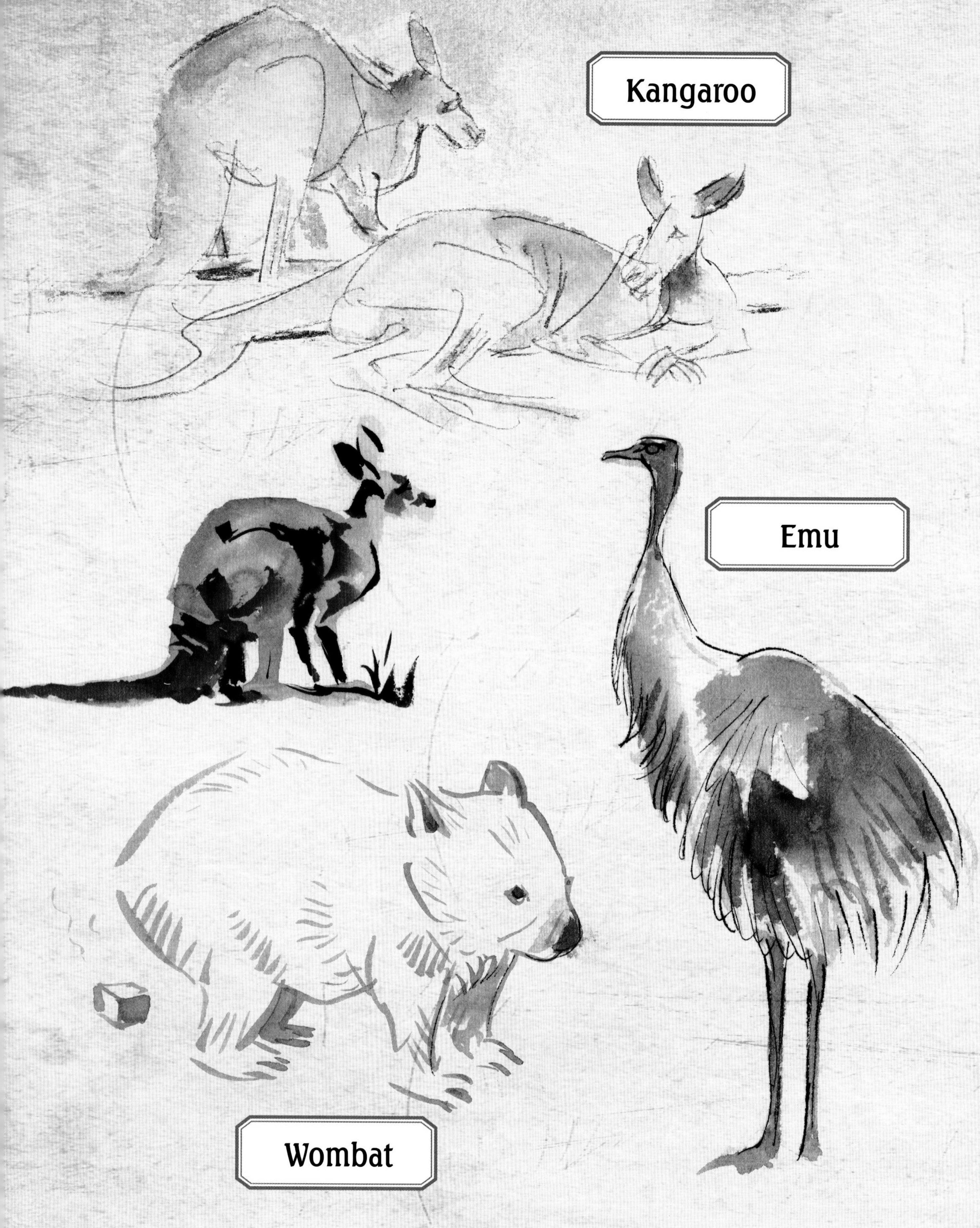
Kangaroo
Emu
Wombat

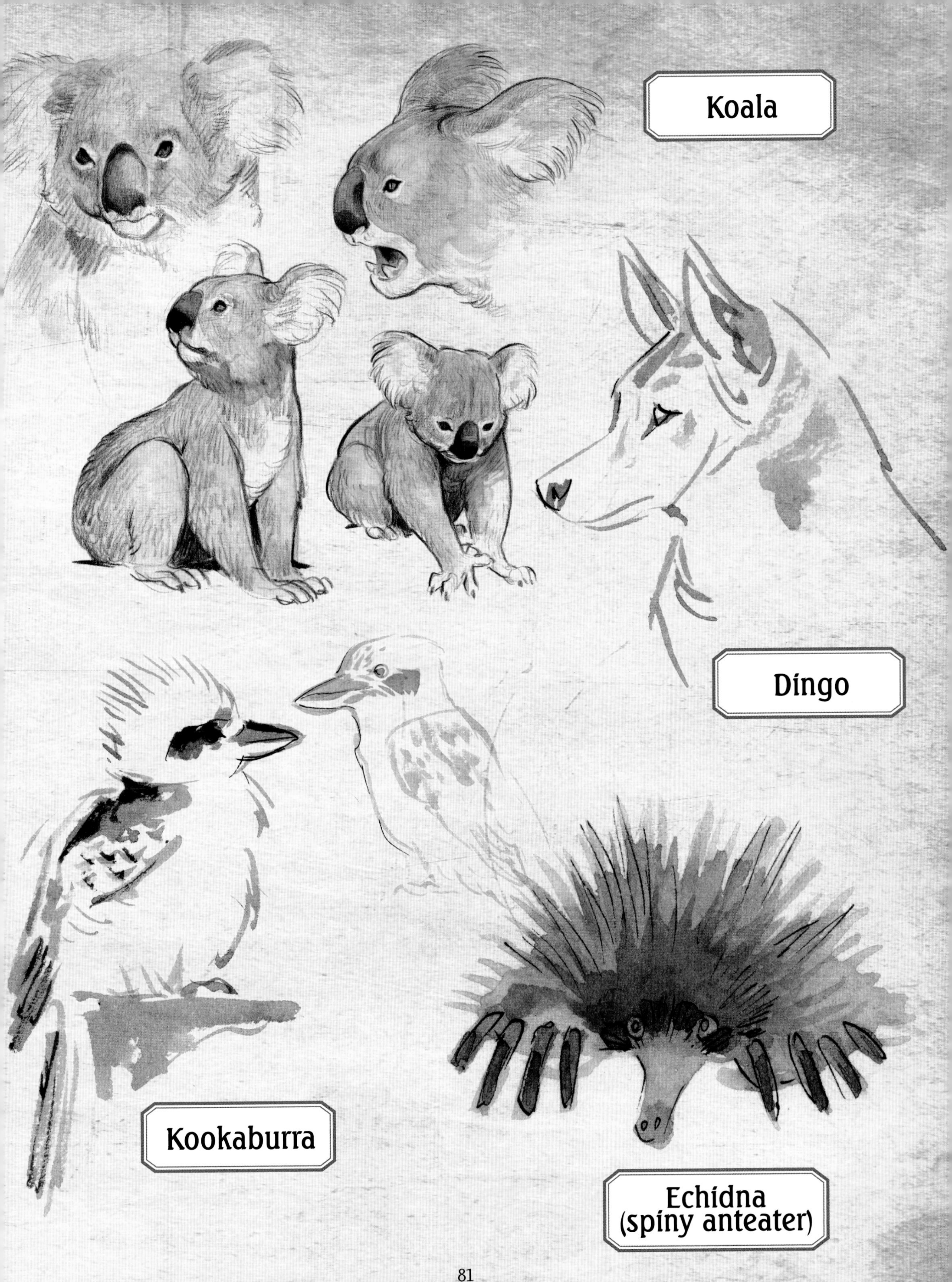
Koala
Dingo
Kookaburra
Echidna
(spiny anteater)

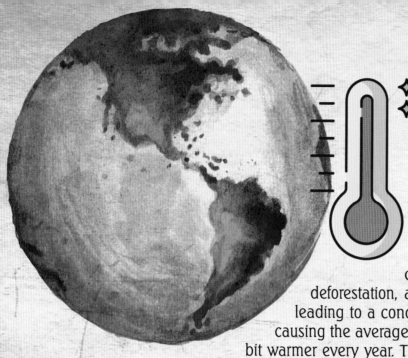

CLIMATE CHANGE and GLOBAL WARMING

Every living thing on Earth relies on the planet's delicate climate, and even small changes can disrupt the fragile balance of nature. Humans are slowly damaging the climate through greenhouse gas pollution, deforestation, and industrial expansion. These actions are leading to a condition known as **"Global Warming,"** and it is causing the average temperature of the Earth to grow just a little bit warmer every year. This rise in temperature may seem small, but over time it can cause big changes to the world's climate.

HOTTER DAYS: 2016 was the hottest year ever recorded, with the ten hottest years in history occurring since 1998. In the past few years, heatwave records have been broken and the Bureau of Meteorology has been forced to add purple and magenta colors to the forecast map to now account for **temperatures up to 54°C (130°F)!**

MELTING ICE AND RISING SEA LEVELS: The higher temperatures are slowly melting glaciers and ice caps all over the world. Not only does this mean less land for many animals like polar bears and penguins, but it also means more water in our oceans which causes sea levels to rise, threatening low-lying islands and coastal cities.

MORE EXTREME WEATHER EVENTS: Brushfires, hurricanes, droughts, and floods are becoming more frequent and more severe. 2020 saw the largest number of tropical storms in a single year, and the second most hurricanes after the record-setting storm season of 2005. Similarly, 2019-2020 saw the most territory destroyed by wildfires, with over **a quarter-million square kilometers** burned in Australia, Siberia, California, and the Amazon rainforest alone.

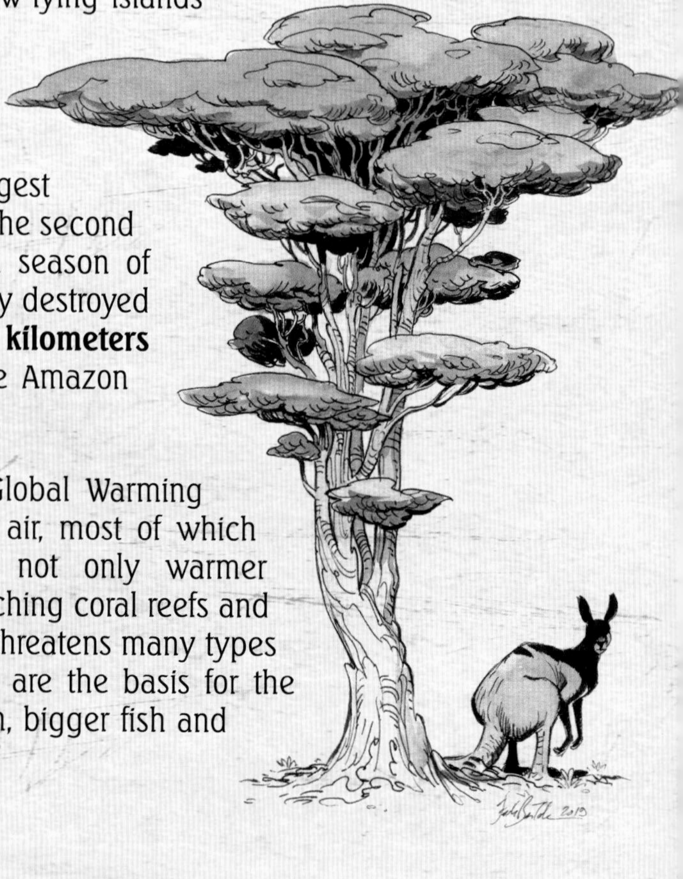

ACIDIFYING OCEANS: One of the byproducts of Global Warming is an increase in carbon dioxide (CO_2) in the air, most of which is absorbed by the oceans making them not only warmer but more acidic. These warmer waters are bleaching coral reefs and creating stronger tropical storms. Rising acidity threatens many types of sea life, including the tiny crustaceans that are the basis for the entire marine food chain. Without those tiny fish, bigger fish and mammals have less to eat.

Sadly, the effects of Global Warming are being felt very strongly across Australia.

RISING TEMPERATURES AND WILDFIRES:
From June of 2019 through May of 2020, record-breaking temperatures combined with months of drought fueled a series of massive brushfires that destroyed more than **27 million square acres** of bush, forest, and parklands. Almost **3 billion animals were killed or displaced by these fires.** Even those that survived the flames were faced with starvation, dehydration, and other desperate predators. Scientists with the World Weather Attribution group concluded that Global Warming raised the chances of the hot, dry weather that caused these fires by at least 30%.

EXTINCTION RISK: Scientists estimate that one in six species is at risk of extinction because of climate change. To survive, plants, animals and birds confronted with climate change have two options: move or adapt. But considering how quickly the climate is changing, it's not possible for some species to adapt quickly enough. During the 2019-2020 brushfires, more than **100 threatened species were pushed to the brink of extinction, with nearly 80% of their homes affected.**

DROUGHT: Changes to rainfall patterns, increasingly frequent heat waves, and extreme weather make it more and more difficult for farmers to raise livestock and grow produce. This reduces the availability of food, making it more expensive to buy.

CORAL BLEACHING AND COASTAL EROSION:
Australia's Great Barrier Reef was once considered "The Rainforest of the Sea," providing food, shelter, and oxygen for billions of organisms. Yet **more than half of its 130,000 square miles have died in the past 25 years** with little sign of recovery. Likewise, rising sea levels and increasingly frequent storms have caused a growing amount of erosion along Australia's coastline, wearing away wildlife territory as well as human residential properties.

TEN WAYS YOU CAN FIGHT GLOBAL WARMING:

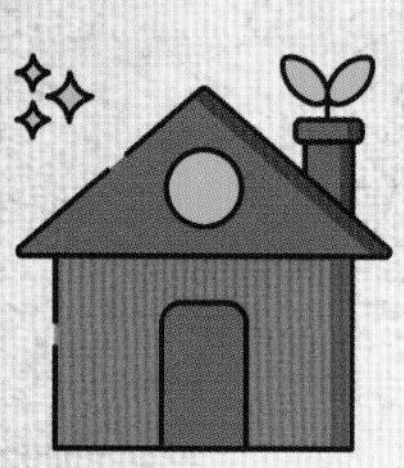

1. **Switch to renewable sources of energy,** such as solar and wind, and less fossil fuels like coal and oil.

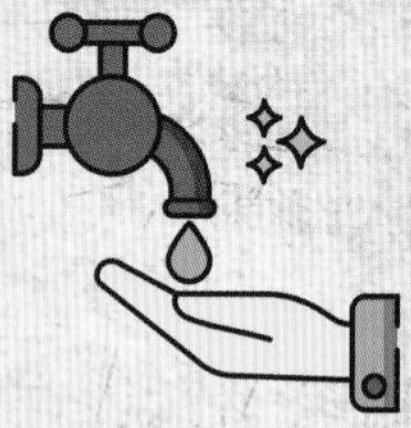

2. **Save water.** Turn off the faucet when brushing your teeth, take shorter showers, and be mindful of how much energy it takes to treat, heat, and pump that water into your home.

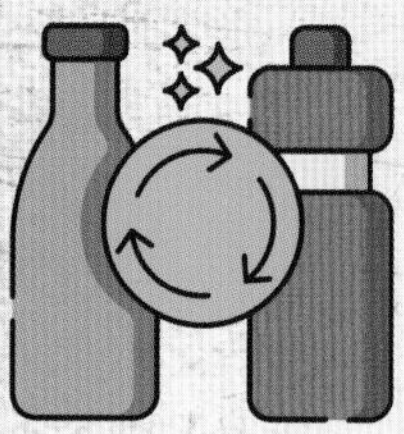

3. **Reduce waste** by reusing or recycle anything that can be used again. Plastic water bottles and excess packaging that is just thrown away are filling the landfills and oceans with waste.

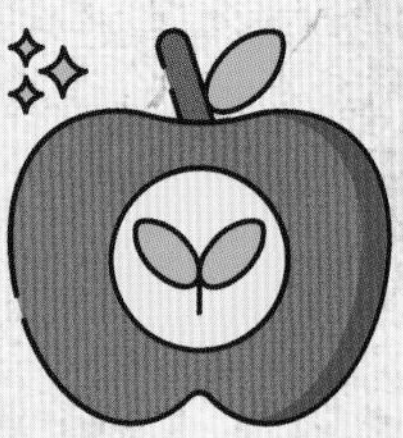

4. **Eat smart (and eat less meat).** A lot of energy is spent growing, processing, and packaging food, 40% of which tends to end up in a landfill. Livestock products require the most energy to raise, process, and package, so eating meat-free meals can make a big difference.

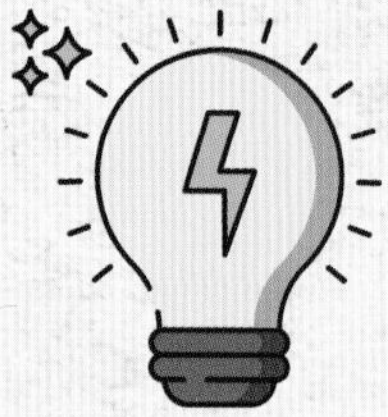

5. **Be energy-efficient:** Turn off the lights and electrical devices when you aren't using them, and switch to LED light bulbs which require 80 less energy. (They last longer too, reducing waste in landfills.)

6. **Wear a sweater in winter and lighter clothes in the summer** to reduce energy used for heating or air conditioning.

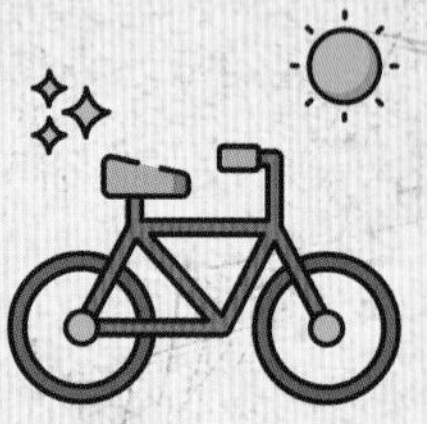

7. **Use mass transit** to reduce the number of cars polluting the air. Or better yet, **bike or walk** if it's close enough!

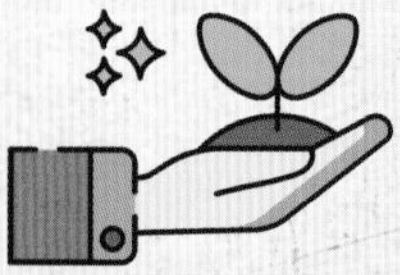

8. **Plant trees** and protect natural resources to reduce your "carbon footprint."

9. **Support "green" businesses** that use and promote clean energy.

10. **Speak up!** Talk to your friends and family to encourage them to protect the environment, too!

For more information on Climate Change and how you can help protect Australian wildlife, visit these websites and organizations:

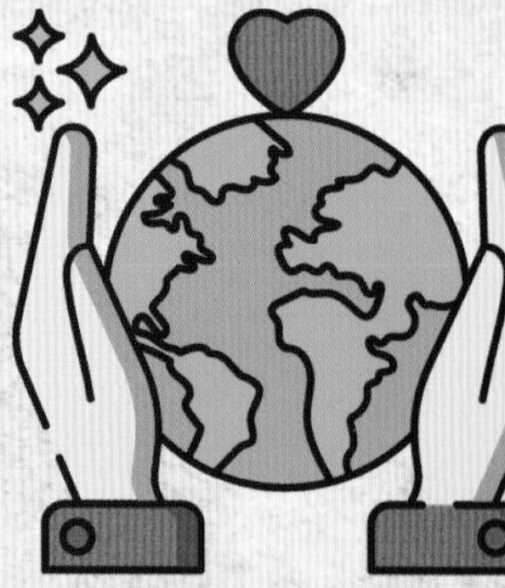

AUSTRALIA ZOO WILDLIFE WARRIORS
https://wildlifewarriors.org.au/

WORLD WILDLIFE FUND AUSTRALIA
https://www.wwf.org.au/